THE PALL MALL DIRECTIVE

PATRICK SEAN KELLY is a former senior UK police officer turned international security and resilience adviser. Over a career spanning three decades, he served in complex operational, investigative, and strategic leadership roles before moving into security-sector reform and capacity-building across West Africa and Europe. His work has focused on integrity in policing, crisis preparedness, and the rule of law.

Patrick is Director of SafehousePro UK and KelSec Global, where he advises governments, institutions, and communities on resilience, emergency preparedness, and strategic security planning. He is also a regular contributor to national and international discussions on civil protection, community resilience, and geopolitical risk.

Drawing on real-world experience from conflict-affected and politically sensitive environments, Patrick's writing blends authenticity, moral complexity, and a deep understanding of the human dimensions of security. The Pall Mall Directive is his debut novel in the Strategic Shadows series.

THE PALL MALL DIRECTIVE

Book One of the Strategic Shadows Series

Patrick Sean Kelly

KelSec Publishing

Published by KelSec Publishing, an imprint of KelSec Global Ltd.

ISBN (Paperback): 978-1-9193959-0-6
ISBN (eBook): 978-1-9193959-1-3

Printed in the United Kingdom.

“Home is the first sanctuary
and the last truth.”

For my family–
Your love anchors me.
Your faith lifts me.
Every story I tell begins with you.

PROLOGUE

Somewhere off the coast of West Africa–nine years before the day everything changed–a man knelt in the dark and let the sea decide whether he lived long enough to regret what he was about to do.

The small cabin groaned with every rising wave. Diesel fumes hung in the air, sharp and metallic, mixing with the brine that seeped through rusted seams in the hull. The floor pitched beneath him, steady in its violence, as though the ocean had chosen this night to test the strength of steel and men alike.

Michael Sillah pressed a hand to the cold bulkhead, steadying himself. Breath gathered tight in his chest. He had made impossible decisions before, but never one that carried a weight like this – one that felt carved into the years that lay ahead, waiting to be lived or endured.

Outside, boots thudded across the deck. Muted voices. The scrape of something heavy being dragged. Orders delivered too quietly to be official. Too purposeful to be panicked.

Michael closed his eyes.

He could still feel the pulse of the city he had left behind–the smoke, the riots, the shouts echoing through streets that had once been home. He could still see the faces of those who trusted him to help, not abandon. But the coup had rewritten every rule. Loyalty had become currency. Safety had become myth. And trust… trust had become a luxury no one could afford.

He opened the metal case on the floor beside him.

Inside lay the reason he was here – the reason the night had turned so dark it felt biblical.

If he handed it over, people would die.

If he kept it, people would die.

But only one path allowed him to choose who.

The cabin door burst open, spilling lantern light across the suffocating gloom. A silhouette filled the doorway–broad-shouldered, armed, impatient.

"Time," the man said.

Michael rose slowly, the decision settling over him like ash.
There was no right choice.
Only the one he could live with – and the one he could never return from.
He picked up the case.
Stepped forward.
And the night swallowed the rest.

Chapter 1

THE PALL MALL DIRECTIVE

"The child who is not embraced by the village
will burn it down to feel its warmth."
– African Proverb

The whiskey wasn't his, but it was there.

Neat. Single malt. Irish, which made him smile despite himself. Whoever had brought it knew their audience.

Michael Sillah sat alone beneath the cracked fresco of the Travellers Club's central dome, watching dust swirl in a shaft of October light. Pall Mall outside was damp and colourless, filled with the purposeful indifference of Londoners in coats too expensive for the weather they were designed to ignore.

Inside, time moved like cigar smoke. Men with medals on their chests and regrets in their spines shuffled papers that didn't matter. The same men who sent other men to die. The kind who'd once pointed him towards West Africa and now wouldn't meet his eyes.

The contract was gone.

Nine months of diplomacy, diligence, training plans, backchannel talks with reformers in Liberia and diplomats in Banjul. Erased in one call. No explanation. No appeal. Just a new strategic direction. Regional partners. Local ownership.

Bullshit.

He'd seen the spreadsheet version of that story. A thin veneer over the rot.

Michael didn't drink. Not often. Not this early. But the glass was there, and it looked like goodbye.

He stared into it.

He didn't see whiskey. He saw a convoy of white Land Cruisers crawling through Kissy in the heat. He saw the warped blue of the Atlantic. He saw a woman on a rooftop, arms folded, eyes full of warning. He saw a red folder he'd once refused to open.

He saw a man he almost became.

He was thirty-seven years old. Born in Sierra Leone. Raised in Surrey. He'd had the best of everything. Boarding school. Debating medals. A place at Cambridge deferred then ignored because he'd joined the police instead. A black lad in blue. First in his intake. First in firearms. First on the scene at the wrong time, more than once.

And now, no badge. No contract. No Africa. Just this drink, this club, and this chair where they sat men like him to be forgotten politely.

"You're in Charles Dance's chair."

The voice was cool and British in that specific way only ex-intelligence officers manage anymore. The man who spoke was tall, pale, and absolutely not a stranger.

Michael didn't look up. "He won't mind."

"No. But the waiter might. He's terrified you're going to light a cigar."

"I don't smoke."

"Neither does Dance."

The man slid into the seat opposite. A navy suit, sharply tailored, with cufflinks that cost more than Michael's first car. His presence didn't ask permission. It declared outcome.

"Penrose," he said, as if the name came with clearance.

Michael raised an eyebrow. "You're late."

"I'm always early. You're just impatient."

Penrose nodded at the untouched drink. "You used to favour rum."

"I still do."

"Irish whiskey's a peace offering. From us."

"There is no 'us.'"

"There will be."

Michael exhaled slowly, as if deflating something coiled inside.

"You came to rub it in?" he asked. "Or recruit me for something equally doomed?"

"Neither." Penrose placed a slim manila folder on the table. Not pushed – placed. "I came to redirect you."

Michael stared at the folder but didn't touch it.

"You're upset," Penrose said. "Expected. They gutted your deployment and didn't even send flowers. But you're not a man who stays upset. You're a man who looks for the next breach in the wall."

"You mean the next betrayal."

"I mean opportunity. But I admire your consistency."

Michael glanced at the folder. "That for me?"

"Only if you want it."

"You always play the enigmatic bastard?"

"Only when it works."

Michael chuckled, just once. Then, finally, he opened the folder.

Three photos. One map. Two names circled in red.

He froze.

The first name was Samuel Jalloh.

The second was a face he hadn't seen in two years. A journalist. Female. Beautiful. Brilliant. Dangerous in all the right ways.

Mariama.

Her brother – Jalloh – had been a known quantity. Once a rebel fighter. Now a police commander. Reformed on paper, unreformed in reality. Tied to half a dozen regional power plays, from Monrovia to Conakry.

But Mariama?

She'd been the one to warn him. To ask him, gently, not to stay. To kiss him like it mattered. To disappear when things got too close to true.

"You're using ghosts," he said quietly.

"We're reviving old legends."

Michael looked up. "How long have you been watching me?"

Penrose smiled. "Since before they sent you home."

"I wasn't sent. I left."

Penrose said nothing.

Michael closed the folder and leaned back. He studied the ceiling again, as if the plaster cherubs had answers.

"She said if I stayed, I'd drown," he murmured.

"She wasn't wrong."

He looked at Penrose. "So why go back?"

"Because now you know how to swim."

The plane banked left over the Freetown peninsula and dropped through a ragged veil of mist that smelled – even through the sealed cabin – like salt, smoke, and time.

Michael hadn't expected the physical reaction.

His chest tightened. His palms itched. His pulse stumbled like a man chasing old shadows through gravel.

He was home. And he wasn't.

From above, the coastline was jagged and green, teeth clenched into the Atlantic. Clusters of corrugated rooftops shimmered in the haze. The hills were hunched like men listening for gunfire. And everywhere – the unforgiving gold of laterite earth.

Touchdown was hard. No welcome.

The airport was stripped-down and sun-bleached. A row of armed guards blinked against the heat. Their camouflage was crisp but didn't fit. One of them chewed gum with the resolve of a man daring the day to test him.

A tall figure waited at the bottom of the steps.

No clipboard. No name.

Just a laminated red circle, taped to a broken iPad.

Michael descended slowly, scanning the space. The air hit him like hot cloth – damp, metallic, unmistakable. Sierra Leone wasn't a smell, it was a temperature of memory. As soon as it touched you, the past began to drip.

He reached the man. No handshake. No words. Just a curt nod and a jerk of the chin toward a black Toyota Prado with dust-choked tyres and no licence plates.

The driver didn't speak. Not even a greeting. Just turned the ignition and pulled out, weaving with quiet confidence through checkpoints, potholes, goats, and boda-bodas like a man who'd done this dance in dreams.

Michael said nothing. The Prado's air conditioning was a joke – something between a cough and a wheeze. Sweat gathered between his shoulder blades like an old secret returning to whisper.

The journey took forty-five minutes, though it felt like time didn't function properly here.

Past Lungi. Across the ferry landing. Into the pulse of Freetown, where chaos wasn't the opposite of order, it was the order.

The city clung to the peninsula like a drunk to a barstool – refusing to fall, despite everything.

Children hawked SIM cards through car windows. Market stalls overflowed with vegetables next to piles of burning plastic. Somewhere nearby, a mosque call blurred with hip-hop through a cracked speaker. Life was loud, urgent, unrepentant.

Then, suddenly – silence.

The Prado turned off the main road into Murray Town, following a track so narrow even the stray dogs hesitated. The tyres crunched over broken shells and rusted nails. A faded UN poster peeled off a wall. The electricity lines were knotted like a child's nightmare.

The safehouse didn't look like safety.

Two stories. No signage. Bars on the windows. The kind of place that looked like it had secrets and no patience for yours.

The gates creaked open with a groan like someone waking unwillingly.

The driver killed the engine.

Still no words.

Michael stepped out.

The Prado reversed and disappeared down the alley, already a memory.

Inside, the house smelled of bleach, mildew, and something faintly medical. It had clearly been cleaned recently – but in the way a crime scene is cleaned: functional, not comforting.

The hallway was narrow and hot. A ceiling fan clicked with the weary rhythm of something close to death. On one wall, a faded poster of the ECOWAS emblem had been half torn, revealing an older, bullet-pocked surface beneath.

Michael passed through the rooms one by one. No surveillance. No decoration. One broken fridge. One working socket. A metal trunk in the bedroom, padlocked but empty.

No fridge magnet notes. No food. No faces.

Just the essentials. And one unexpected touch.

On the table, in the main room, sat a plastic bag – translucent and sweating under the heat. Inside:

A basic mobile phone

A SIM card in a torn paper sleeve

250,000 Leones in rubber-banded notes

A small metal key

A folded piece of thick, off-white paper

Michael unfolded the note. No letterhead. No signature. The handwriting was slow, almost elegant – like someone who had taught themselves to write in ink before ever typing a text.

Do not trust the fixer. He plays both sides.

He read it again.

A whisper of wind passed through the window grille. A rooster screamed in the distance – as if to warn.

Michael stood still for a long moment.

Then made tea on a rusting camping stove wedged on a concrete shelf in the toilet, where the plumbing barely bothered pretending.

He sipped in silence, barefoot, cross-legged on the floor beside the folder Penrose had given him.

Jalloh. Mariama. Koidu.

He flipped through the pages again.

Satellite imagery. Financial flows. Grinning men with expensive watches and blood on their hands.

A mining concession, revoked and reinstated. A French telecoms contract with the wrong backers. A dead man in Monrovia with Michael's old business card in his wallet.

He didn't blink.

Rain began.

Not a drizzle. A deluge. The kind that arrived with drama – sudden, biblical, drumming on the zinc roof with a fury that made it feel like the gods were arguing above.

That's when the knock came.

Three short, sharp raps.

Michael froze. He'd locked the door. Twice.

He scanned the room. No weapon. No blade. No baton.

The only thing he could grab was the steel spoon from the tea.

He set it down. Pointless.

The knock came again.

Slower this time. Deliberate. Like someone who knew they were expected.

Michael approached the door, slow and silent. To the left of the frame, he peered through the peep hole.

No one.

No vehicle.

No movement.

Just the dark outline of a man in a long coat, collar turned up, standing in the thick curtain of rain with no umbrella, no haste, and no fear.

Michael opened the door two inches.

The man stepped in like mist.

The man stepped inside like fog – quiet, confident, and cold in the way only someone dangerous by nature could be. The rain clung to his coat in beads, soaking the frayed collar of a charcoal trench he hadn't bothered to button. No umbrella. No urgency. No fear.

Michael didn't offer a handshake. He didn't move.

The fixer peeled off his coat slowly, deliberately, revealing a linen shirt clinging to wiry muscle and tattoos that ran from his forearm to his collarbone – tribal, maybe, or just designed to look that way. His presence was silent and suffocating, like a room where someone had died recently.

He hung the coat on the back of a chair, then sat in it backwards, straddling it with the casual arrogance of a man who'd once tortured someone in that exact position.

Michael crossed his arms, keeping his body between the door and the man.

"You're late," he said.

The fixer smiled – not a pleasant one. "You're early."

The accent was soft Krio, but worn down by French and something older. A voice you didn't forget if you'd heard it on the wrong end of a radio.

Michael nodded at the bag on the table. "You leave the welcome pack?"

"I leave warnings. Not gifts."

"You play both sides."

The fixer studied him, eyes dark and impassive. "Only the sides that pay."

"And when they stop paying?"

"Then I change the game."

Michael didn't blink. "You have a name?"

The fixer's eyes lingered on him, measuring.

"They call me Demba."

"Real name?"

"Does it matter?"

Michael walked around the table slowly. "Only if I need to write it on a gravestone."

Demba chuckled, low and hollow. "Still British, eh? Always believing a name gives you control."

"No. Just direction."

A silence settled – not awkward, but loaded, like a prelude.

Then Demba reached into his coat pocket.

Michael tensed.

The man pulled out a plain mobile phone – the kind used by dealers, informants, and men who never intended to explain themselves. He placed it on the table, screen down.

"No apps," Demba said. "No memory card. No GPS. It will ring once. When it does, you answer. Nothing more."

"Who's calling?"

Demba stood and walked to the sink, pouring himself a glass of water from a warm bottle. He drank like he'd just crossed a desert.

Michael waited.

When Demba returned, he didn't sit.

"Jalloh thinks you're here to negotiate," he said finally.

"I'm not."

"He's already planning your welcome parade. Guns. Speeches. Maybe a staged arrest to make it look like progress."

"I don't stage things."

"That's your problem."

Michael stepped closer. "You know what he did in Pujehun?"

"I know what he covered up."

"And Mariama?"

That name landed like a weapon. Demba froze – just a flicker in the shoulder. But it was enough.

"She's not part of this," he said flatly.

"She always was."

"She's out."

"No one gets out."

Demba leaned forward. "You still think you're here to save people?"

Michael's jaw tightened. "I think people like you need watching."

"I'm not the one who got kicked out of the country for refusing to play."

"No – you just change flags and keep the blood off your boots."

Demba's face remained still, but something flickered in the eyes – not anger, not pride. Something colder.

"I've survived longer than anyone else in this game," he said. "Because I know when to lie, when to listen, and when to disappear."

Michael stepped back. "So disappear."

Demba didn't move. "You think you're here because of your CV? Because of the training modules you wrote for Monrovia or the gender review in The Gambia?"

He leaned in, voice lower.

"You're here because you're inconvenient. And dangerous. And useful – for now. The moment that changes, you'll vanish like your last deployment."

Michael flinched.

Demba smiled. "Ah. So they didn't tell you why the contract was pulled?"

Michael said nothing.

"Thought not."

Rain lashed the roof again – loud, persistent, drowning the silence.

Demba walked to the door but didn't open it. He turned.

"You'll get coordinates tomorrow. Don't bring anything you want to keep."

He reached into his pocket one last time and placed something in Michael's hand. Small. Cold. Heavy.

By the time Michael looked down, Demba was already gone – a blur in the rain.

It was a coin.

Old. Scarred.

On one side: a lion. On the other: a broken chain.

Not currency. Not a souvenir.

A message.

Michael didn't sleep that night.

He sat in the dark, listening to the rain, the coin resting on the table like a verdict.

The phone didn't ring.

Not yet.

The rain had stopped around 3:00 a.m., but the silence it left behind was worse.

Michael hadn't moved for hours. He sat on the edge of the low bed, one bare foot pressed against the cool tiled floor, the other tucked beneath him like a soldier waiting for a breach. The red folder lay beside him, unopened since midnight. The coin sat on the table, glinting dully under the single naked bulb. The burner phone, still silent, rested beside it like a coiled trap.

The house groaned occasionally – not with ghosts, but with memory.

He was still trying to breathe it all in. The ache in his ribs that came not from exertion but from memory. Freetown at night did that. It had a way of sitting on your chest.

At 04:17, the phone buzzed. Not rang – buzzed.

He stared at it like a snake had just slithered across the table.

Once.

Twice.

Then silence.

Michael picked it up and pressed answer. He said nothing.

A woman's voice, crisp and clipped, slid down the line like surgical steel.

"Mr Sillah. Confirm your readiness."

He didn't respond at first. The voice was familiar, though he couldn't place it. Southern English. Public school, but tempered by intelligence work – someone who had trained herself out of sounding too posh. Someone used to control.

"Who is this?" he asked finally.

"We don't use names. Not on open lines. Especially not this one."

He looked down at the coin. "Then why call?"

"To give you a window. One time only."

"I already have the file."

"That's the bait. Now comes the hook."

Michael rubbed his eyes. "You're Consortium."

"Not exactly. We serve similar interests."

"And what are those?"

"West Africa stable enough to trade, but unstable enough to require insurance."

He laughed, dry and low. "That's not a mission. That's a business model."

"Exactly."

She let it sit. A silence so sharp it hummed.

"You'll receive a location drop at 05:30. Go alone. No phones, no contacts, no comms."

He shook his head. "You know I was deported from here. You know I'm being watched."

"Yes. That's why we chose you."

"How comforting."

"Don't be comforted. Be useful."

Her tone softened – not warmth, exactly, but something that echoed memory.

"We're not asking for heroics, Michael. Just clarity."

He felt something shift in his chest.

"You know me?"

"We know enough. We know why you left. We know why you stayed silent. We know who you couldn't save."

That was a step too far.

"Say her name," he growled.

"No."

That silence again – but now it was intimate. Strategic.

"You'll recognise the scent soon enough. Things are moving in the east. People with long memories and short tempers. You're not being asked to fight them. You're being asked to find the shape of the fire before it burns the forest."

The line went dead.

Michael didn't move. He just sat.

Then, deliberately, he dropped the phone into the tin basin under the sink and poured bleach over it until it hissed and bubbled.

He washed with bottled water. The generator coughed out its last breath as he laced his boots.

He dressed in what he had: canvas trousers, a linen shirt that still smelled faintly of ironed starch and old briefing rooms. He found a piece of cord in the back pocket of his rucksack and threaded the coin onto it, tying it around his neck, just below the collarbone.

For a moment, he stood in the middle of the room.

Eyes closed.

He could feel her again.

Mariama. In a jeep with no seatbelts. Laughing at a UN inspector's pompous questions. Arguing over breakfast about the ethics of bribes for borehole security.

Then screaming.

Then gone.

He opened his eyes.

At 05:36, the sun had begun to smear orange across the rooftops of Murray Town. The heat returned like an apology. He stepped into the street without a sound.

The route they'd indicated was clear but dangerous – an old quarry road out near Goderich, now home to squatters and silence. He moved with purpose, but not speed. No tail. No watchers.

Only the past.

The meeting point was a half-collapsed colonial structure, wrapped in ivy and half-swallowed by the hillside. A man stood at the entrance. Unmarked clothing. Watchful eyes. The way his hands rested near his hips told Michael everything he needed to know.

"Right on time," the man said.

Michael didn't respond. He waited.

The man opened a steel door. "We've kept the light on."

Inside was no safer than outside – just quieter.

The room was stripped bare except for a single desk, a sealed laptop, and a black case the size of a football. No insignia. No flags. No welcome.

Michael sat.

The man stood behind him, motionless.

He opened the laptop.

No password. No splash screen. Just a folder named KUMBA.

Inside: photographs.

Satellite stills. Heat maps. A river crossing in the northeast. A known smuggler's compound in Guinea. A burnt-out church near Zimmi.

And then – her.

Mariama.

Hair shorter. Eyes harder. Standing behind a podium with the emblem of a minor NGO Michael had never heard of – the Foresight Initiative.

The timestamp was 23 days ago.

He stared at the image for a long time.

Then he spoke.

"She's alive."

"Yes," said the man behind him.

"Why hasn't she contacted me?"

"Maybe she thought you were dead. Or maybe she hoped you were."

Michael turned. "Why show me this now?"

"Because whether she likes it or not, she's part of this."

Michael looked back at the screen. "You're using her."

"No. But others are. And if they succeed, Sierra Leone won't be a failed state. It'll be a memory."

Michael shut the laptop.

"What do you need me to do?"

The man's reply was immediate.

"Disappear. Then reappear exactly where they don't want you."

"And after that?"

The man smiled faintly. "Rewrite the directive."

Outside, the sun broke fully over the hills.

Michael walked slowly to the edge of the road and looked out over the city. He could see the port cranes in the distance. Hear the faint rattle of a poda-poda radio. Smell grilled fish and gasoline.

His land. His ghosts.

And finally – his mission.
He pulled the coin from under his shirt and let it rest in his palm.
The lion stared back.

Chapter 2

GHOSTS IN THE SMOKE

"When the roots of a tree begin to decay,
it spreads death to the branches."
– African proverb (Nigerian origin)

The dawn heat came early in Freetown, heavy with the smell of salt, sweat, and something less definable – ambition maybe, or regret. Michael stood at the balcony edge of the crumbling safehouse, barefoot, coffee in hand, watching the city stir below like a half-remembered dream trying to retake form.

Fishermen haggled over diesel at the roadside. A boy herded goats with a stick and a football chant. A woman washed clothes in rhythmic slaps against a concrete basin, humming a song he didn't recognise but felt in his bones. Life resumed in vivid fragments, and yet to Michael it all felt slightly askew – like returning to an old film, but the scenes were out of order.

Behind him, the red folder lay where he'd left it. Open now. Read twice.

The names inside weren't a list. They were a map – of people, decisions, betrayals. Some were scratched out, others underlined. But one was circled in fading blue ink.

Abigail Conteh.

It hit him like a sucker punch. Not because it was unexpected – but because it made too much sense. A name he hadn't heard in seven years. Former journalist. Mariama's colleague, maybe more. Vanished after a Ministry leak and an attempted arrest that turned into a footnote in a human rights report. The kind of person who didn't just disappear – she was disappeared.

Michael sipped the coffee. Bitter, thin, boiling. Like truth in this country.

He paced the cracked tile floor, glancing again at the open folder. Someone had kept meticulous notes – surveillance logs, interview transcripts, intelligence cross-referenced with old case files. Mariama's influence was all over it, from the shorthand used in the margins to the deliberate redactions. Whatever she'd uncovered had been dangerous enough to bury her. And now, it seemed, dangerous enough to resurrect.

The burner phone buzzed across the table.

Unknown number. Local prefix.

He answered without speaking.

"Michael Sillah," said a voice like velvet dragged over gravel. "Still chasing ghosts?"

He didn't reply. The voice was male, older, familiar but worn down by time or hard use.

"You opened the folder."

Still no reply.

"Then you know the name. Lumley Market. Before noon. Come alone."

Click.

Michael stared at the phone a second longer than necessary. Then stood, walked back to the room, and slipped the red folder beneath the floorboards where the wood was already loosened. He'd seen the same folder system used in the Balkans, and once in Haiti – a dead drop disguised as paranoia.

He dressed slowly. Nothing tactical, nothing that screamed foreign. Local shirt, worn trousers, trainers with dust still clinging to the laces from his arrival. He hesitated before tucking the coin into his sock – not superstition. Insurance.

The heat had intensified by the time he stepped onto the street. The air buzzed with morning commerce. Mango sellers called out in Krio, taxis blasted horns as punctuation, and roosters screamed like unpaid prophets. The streets were slick with last night's rain, already steaming, giving the illusion of smoke rising from the gutters.

He walked. Not too fast. Not too slow. Just another face in the mosaic of the city.

The fixer hadn't returned. Demba was either being careful or being watched. Michael wasn't sure which unnerved him more. The absence felt intentional – staged, even. A vacuum in the script.

He felt it first at the corner of Wilkinson Road. A presence. Not seen – sensed.

A woman paused at a kiosk. No phone. No bag. But her eyes were on him a second too long. She lit a cigarette but didn't smoke it. The flame quivered slightly. Her fingers were too steady.

A man crossed the street behind him. Sloppy beard, loose boots. The kind that didn't fit the uniform of the morning. Something about the gait was off – purposeful without purpose.

Michael ducked into a café near Congo Cross, ordered tea he wouldn't drink, and circled out the back exit. His route wasn't random – three right turns and a straight would tell him if he was truly being tailed.

He was.

Good.

That meant someone was taking him seriously.

He passed a makeshift chapel housed in a shipping container. A child outside offered him a wilted flower. He took it, nodded, and placed it on the dashboard of a broken taxi abandoned by the kerb – a minor offering to the city, or perhaps to fate.

At the top of Lumley Market, the city opened up like a throat about to shout.

Fishermen. Traders. Pickpockets. Preachers with megaphones. The smell of fish guts, engine oil, and knockoff perfume. A radio blared highlife from a stall stacked with secondhand shoes.

Michael waited under the broken fan of a palm tree, eyes on the tide. The bustle swirled around him, a living tide of movement and murmurs. He was alone and surrounded, invisible and exposed.

"Still chasing ghosts," the voice had said.

He was done chasing.

Now he was hunting.

Freetown's noise had a rhythm, but tonight it stuttered. A beat was missing.

Michael moved through the Lumley chaos with his collar up and his instincts wired tight. The contact never showed. No signal. No brush pass. Just a roiling market of voices and smoke and counterfeit goods. The ground felt slightly off-balance beneath his feet, like the city was holding its breath.

He stayed an extra twenty minutes, feigning interest in a stall selling knock-off designer watches and belts, the kind smuggled in by Lebanese middlemen and sold to NGO expats looking for cheap status. He drifted from vendor to vendor, half-heartedly haggling for roasted cashews while his eyes scanned the crowd. But whoever had called him was either spooked–or never intended to come.

A taillight flickered at the edge of his vision. Same motorbike. Too many turns in tandem. Too many pauses at junctions where no pause was needed.

He crossed over to the other side of the market, letting a group of church women in printed wax fabric absorb him for cover. Then he turned into a side alley, slipped past a vendor selling grilled plantain, and doubled back.

The bike was gone.

Sloppy tailing or deliberate performance?

The market closed in behind him with a wall of sound–shouted prices, diesel engines, a sermon from a tinny speaker, the boom of Afrobeats from a bar three doors down. He exhaled slowly, pressing through a clot of taxi drivers haggling over fuel prices. The sky above had turned the colour of gunmetal. Rain threatened, but hadn't yet come.

Back on Wilkinson Road, the air was thicker. As he approached the safehouse, the hairs on his arms lifted.

The front door was unlocked.

He paused, hand hovering an inch from the wood. The lock bore faint scratches–not enough to break, but enough to check. Someone had tested the resistance. A message, perhaps.

He entered slowly, silent as breath.

Everything was in its place–except Demba.

His satchel still hung on the back of the rickety chair. The folder of contact numbers sat open, untouched. A bottle of Star beer sat sweating condensation beside the bed, half-full. But the man himself had vanished. No note. No sound. Just the open window and the faint scent of sweat and metal.

Michael crouched and ran his fingers along the tiles. A wet boot print. Not Demba's.

He moved to the small kitchenette, checked the drawers. The burner phone was where he'd left it. But now it buzzed once, faint and insect-like. A single message blinked on the screen. He opened it.

"Pademba breathes. Be ready."

Pademba Road Prison.

He hadn't heard that name in months. Not since the last eruption–when some swore a coup was afoot, and others claimed it was just a riot cooked up by the usual suspects behind the wire. Michael knew better. Prisons were never random. They were pressure cookers with a timetable. When they hissed, it meant someone had turned up the heat.

He walked into the washroom, flicked on the light. The bulb buzzed with fatigue.

The mirror gave him a version of himself he half-recognised–creased forehead, beard at day three, sweat beading under his collar. His eyes, though, remained sharp. Tired, but sharp.

"Where are you, Demba?" he asked the reflection.

He splashed water on his face, ran wet fingers through his hair, then reached for the coin in his pocket and flipped it absent-mindedly. Heads. Again.

The Cotton Tree café hadn't changed.

It still smelled of over-brewed coffee and old ambition. The walls were hung with faded prints of revolutionary slogans long out of fashion. The fans turned like exhausted civil servants–slow, unreliable, groaning through their final duties.

He hadn't set foot there since Mariama's funeral. Abigail had spoken exactly five words to him that day–none of them kind–and then vanished into the fog of institutional dysfunction. He'd respected the silence. But now, it hummed too loud.

He picked the seat in the far corner, back to the wall, where he could see both the door and the kitchen pass-through. Old habits.

There were only a few patrons – two tired-looking NGO types nursing warm bottles of Star, speaking in clipped French, and a woman in faded fatigues flirting half-heartedly with a customs officer at the bar. Background noise, but worth remembering.

A teenage waiter shuffled over, poured him coffee without asking, and shuffled off again. No bill, no eye contact.

The café's old clock ticked louder than seemed plausible.

He scanned the room again. Nothing. But his pulse was up. The silence between seconds had too much weight.

The note arrived under the saucer five minutes later.

He hadn't seen the hand that delivered it.

Cream-coloured, no markings, folded once with a precise crease. No perfume. No smudge. He lifted it, felt the thickness. Slightly embossed paper. Expensive. Old money. Or someone wanting to pretend they were.

He unfolded it with his thumb.

"You know where the rot begins."

Just that. No signature. No time. Just a sentence like a whisper from the grave.

Michael stared at the words.

Rot.

He'd heard it used by diplomats, journalists, development analysts. Always in the abstract. Corruption. Inertia. Broken systems. But this was more personal. This was a scalpel slid under scar tissue.

He turned the paper over. Blank.

For a long moment, he simply sat, the noise of the café muting around him, like cotton in his ears. Then he reached into his coat, took out the coin, and spun it on the saucer.

Heads. As always.

He left the café without finishing the coffee, stepping into the dense twilight. The rain held off, but the air pressed in like a warning.

As he moved past the Cotton Tree itself–older than empires, marked with bullet holes and prayers–he thought of Demba.

Pademba. Abigail. Mariama. The fixer who never fixed. The deal that never quite closed. The note that bled old truth.

He was missing something. But the pieces were shifting too fast to catch.

Behind him, a siren wailed once in the distance–shrill, uncertain–and then was swallowed by the city.

Michael walked on.

He didn't know what was coming.

But it had already begun.

The message was simple: "Four p.m. – Grand Leone Hotel. Balcony bar. Come alone."

Michael didn't like ultimatums, but he disliked silence more.

He arrived early, scanning the compound with the caution of a man who'd once stepped on a landmine – not literally, but close enough to remember the ringing in his ears for years after.

The Grand Leone was a gleaming façade of new wealth–glass, concrete, and promise. An oasis for international consultants, local ministers' mistresses, and expat spooks pretending to be trade envoys. The balcony bar overlooked the Atlantic like a predator watches prey – calm, detached, almost bored.

He took a seat near the edge, where the breeze carried the tang of salt and diesel from the port. Waiters moved like dancers – silent, elegant, eyes always watching. He ordered nothing. He didn't need to.

At 4:03, the man appeared.

Mid-forties, pale linen suit with a West African twist – tailored but unpretentious. No tie. Dark glasses. Clean-shaven. The kind of man who looked forgettable on purpose.

He didn't introduce himself. Just sat, placed a slim black folder on the table, and rested both hands beside it like he was posing for a chessboard portrait.

"You're early," the man said. British, but flattened. Somewhere between Sandhurst and Geneva.

Michael didn't reply.

"You used to be more talkative. At that Goma workshop in 2017–"

"You're not here for nostalgia."

"No," the man said, adjusting his glasses. "I'm here because you're getting close to things people prefer kept distant. And because you haven't entirely burnt your bridges. Yet."

Michael tapped the edge of the table. "Let's talk about Demba."

"He's alive," the man said, and immediately added: "As of this morning."

Michael exhaled. Slowly.

"He was seen at the Pademba perimeter. Not inside, not outside. Just hovering. Three nights ago. Same day the files went missing."

"What files?"

The man opened the folder. Inside were grainy printouts – CCTV stills, blurry ID cards, intake forms. On top, a list of names. About twenty.

"Scheduled transfers. High-risk detainees. All were supposed to be relocated to a temporary holding facility in Kenema. Transfer was delayed. The list disappeared. So did one of the convoy supervisors. Two days later, two bodies turned up near Goderich."

He slid the list across. "Recognise anyone?"

Michael's eyes skimmed the names. Half were unknown. The rest–he'd encountered them in whispers: former soldiers, rebel financiers, a notorious drug mule who'd once claimed diplomatic immunity with a forged Liberian passport.

"What's this got to do with me?" he asked.

The man tilted his head. "You're asking questions no one else is. You're seen as clean. That makes you dangerous. It also makes you useful."

"And what do you get out of this?"

"A buffer. If this turns radioactive, I wasn't here. You were."

Michael leaned back in his chair. The breeze carried the faint sound of a car horn down below. The air tasted of tension and something else – an old, familiar metallic taste of danger.

"I want to see the footage."

The man nodded. "It's in your inbox. Encrypted. Don't forward it. Don't screenshot it. Don't be stupid."

"And Pademba?"

"Something's building there. Two factions inside–one wants chaos. The other wants to cash in on it. And someone's fanning the flames from outside."

"Government?"

The man smiled. "You're still charmingly naïve."

Michael stood.

"Where are you going?" the man asked.

"To follow the rot."

The man gave a small, tight nod. "Then you'd better move quickly. You're not the only one looking for Demba. And you're definitely not the only one he trusted."

That night, Michael walked Freetown's side streets until his feet ached.

The city was quieter than it should've been. The bars were full but subdued, the football games played on mute, the laughter tinged with wariness. Something was shifting under the surface, a pressure no one could name yet but everyone felt in their spine.

Back at the safehouse, the burner phone pinged once.

A photo.

Low-res, time-stamped 03:14 a.m., three nights ago.

Demba, wearing a black rain jacket, standing at a chain-link fence. Behind him, Pademba Road Prison – barely visible in the mist, but unmistakable in silhouette. He looked over his shoulder as though hearing something behind him. And then… nothing.

No follow-up image.

Just that one moment. Frozen.

Michael studied every pixel. Zoomed in. Enlarged the timestamp. Checked shadows. Nothing helped.

He'd seen that look before. It was the look of a man about to run – or about to die.

He saved the image. Locked it behind three layers of encryption. Then, for the first time in days, he poured himself a whiskey – Irish, the good kind – and stared into the glass like it might explain something.

Why Demba had gone to Pademba.

Why the man in linen had chosen now to reach out.

And why his gut told him this wasn't about prison breaks or missing files.

It was about legacy.

And ghosts that refused to stay buried.

"The path does not close for the one who walks with purpose."
– AFRICAN PROVERB

The sun had not yet risen, but Freetown was already moving. It always did – a city that never truly slept, only shifted its rhythm. Michael left the safehouse before dawn, tucking the burner phone into his inner jacket pocket and the strange coin into his palm like a talisman. He needed answers – not whispers or riddles this time, but something solid. Something human.

He walked the length of Kissy Road before the call to prayer. Traders were already setting up under plastic awnings and fraying tarpaulins, unstacking crates of dented tinned milk and sachets of water. A boy ran barefoot across the oily tarmac, balancing a bucket of eggs on his head with the grace of a dancer.

The air was a cocktail of charcoal smoke, damp dust, dried fish, petrol, and something else – an undercurrent of unease he couldn't name but couldn't ignore either. It pressed against the edges of his awareness like a silent siren. He didn't trust it.

His target was a man named Khalifa Bangura, a former senior officer at Pademba Road Prison. Officially, Khalifa had retired two years ago, citing health reasons. But word on the street had always suggested otherwise – whispers of a payoff, a cover-up, a fire that burned more than records.

Michael found him crouched beside a rusting motorcycle near a shuttered mosque in Upgun Turntable, hands buried in grease and elbows twitching in rhythm with the distant drums of traffic.

"You're braver than I thought," Khalifa said without looking up.

"And you're still as paranoid," Michael replied. "Some things never change."

Khalifa glanced at him – a flicker of recognition in tired eyes – then stood and wiped his hands on a rag that looked older than both of them.

They walked side by side through a labyrinth of kiosks and abandoned cars until they reached a video rental shop sealed with corrugated tin. Inside, dust hung like a veil. Shelves leaned under the weight of old VHS tapes – Die Hard, Delta Force, Mandela: The Long Walk. A plastic Jesus bobbled from the counter. Nobody had done business here in a decade.

"Talk," Khalifa said, sitting on an overturned paint bucket. "Quickly."

"I need to know what Demba was chasing," Michael said, lowering his voice. "What got him ghosted?"

Khalifa exhaled like it hurt. "Demba poked where he shouldn't have. Not at drug routes or politics. At files. Old transfer logs. Names that didn't match bodies. Movements without authorisation."

"Block Five?" Michael asked.

Khalifa nodded. "We called it the corridor. It wasn't on any blueprint. No visitors. No guards posted permanently. Just shadows and orders passed down from men who didn't sign papers."

"Who was kept there?"

"No one," Khalifa said flatly. Then added: "And everyone."

Michael narrowed his eyes. "Ghost detainees."

"They weren't criminals," Khalifa whispered. "They were assets. Test cases. Some from other countries. Some from here. All vanished during the chaos after the coup attempt."

"And you knew?"

"I processed them in. Never out."

Silence pulsed between them. Outside, a rooster crowed too late, too close. Inside, a smell of old sweat and regret rose between the tapes.

A knock came at the metal shutter.

Three short. One long.

Khalifa went rigid. "You brought eyes."

"No. I didn't," Michael said. "But someone knew I'd come."

The knock came again. This time slower. Heavier.

Khalifa reached behind the counter and pressed something into Michael's hand. A note. Folded twice. "Go. Now. Out the back. If they ask, I haven't seen you in ten years."

Michael slipped through a side door into a tight alley choked with bins and banana leaves. His shoes squelched on something that smelled of fish and engine oil. Behind him, the shutter screamed open like a wound being torn.

He didn't look back.

By the time he reached Aberdeen Bridge, the city had awoken in full. Market women barked prices with matriarchal authority. Okada bikes buzzed like angry hornets. A bus stalled and backfired near a pile of sodden refuse, and two goats bolted into traffic like prophets fleeing the wrath to come.

Michael ducked into a roadside tea stall. Ordered a ginger tea in a plastic cup that burned his fingers. Sat on a plastic chair with one leg shorter than the others. Then opened the note.

One sentence.

"You're not hunting Demba. You're retracing his path."

Below it: a crude, hand-drawn map. Congo Cross. Ministry of Interior. Marked in red.

Basement Archives.

Michael stared at it until the ink blurred. This wasn't a pursuit. It was a relay. He'd picked up the baton Demba had dropped – or had been forced to drop – and now he was running a leg no one wanted finished.

He took a sip of the tea. Bitter. Spiced. Awakening.

He'd go there tomorrow. Alone.

That night, the rain came hard. As if the sky had been holding its breath since he landed. Thunder rolled down from the hills of Goderich, shaking the tin roofs and trembling the windows. The lights in the safehouse flickered, then died. The generator stayed silent – as if even it had decided to retreat for the night.

Michael sat in the darkness, listening to the rain drum its secrets into the zinc above. He laid the map on the table. Set the coin next to it. Then the phone. A triangle of silent tools. Tools of the trade. Tools of betrayal.

And then, without warning, a smell – cloves and orange oil – filled his nostrils.

Mariama's perfume.

He wasn't alone.

He spun, but the room was empty. Only shadows. Only rain.

But the memory had already opened its door.

"Don't ever mistake silence for safety," she'd once told him, voice low and tired, the last time they'd spoken before she vanished into the system she'd once tried to fix.

He hadn't. Not then. Not now.

A chime broke the moment – the burner phone.

One message.

A photo.

Not Demba.

A corpse. Mutilated. Burned. Dumped by the side of a drainage trench near Jui Junction. Unrecognisable.

Except for one detail.

A coin. Pressed between the lips.

Michael checked his hand. His coin – the one from the safehouse – was still there.

So whose was this?

Not a message. A warning. Or a provocation.

He stood and opened the window. The rain struck him like penance. Far below, Freetown rolled on, electric and unforgiving. Somewhere in that city, a door had opened – and someone had walked through it carrying blood and secrets.

Tomorrow, he would go to the Ministry.

And he would not leave empty-handed.

Chapter 3

THE UNSEEN HAND

"When the roots are deep, there is no reason to fear the wind."
– African proverb

The Ministry of Interior looked like every other monument to post-colonial bureaucracy – weather-stained, fortress-minded, and just paranoid enough to make you feel watched even when alone.

Michael stood at the rear compound gate, where the guards were less diligent and more easily distracted. A crisp handshake, a folded banknote, and a forged maintenance badge later, he was through. No one looked twice at the clipboard in his hand.

Freetown was already wilting under the weight of another humid morning, but inside the Ministry, the temperature dropped. It wasn't the air-conditioning. It was the atmosphere – bureaucratic decay steeped in political survival.

Michael passed a bored receptionist, nodded to a yawning security man, and slipped down a stairwell labeled "RECORDS – ARCHIVE ONLY – STAFF." Paint peeled from the walls like old regrets. The deeper he went, the older the Ministry felt. Like the building had buried its sins under concrete, layer by layer.

He reached the basement landing. The corridor stretched left and right, humming with ancient fluorescent lights that flickered like nervous ticks. A single iron security gate stood half open, its rusted padlock hanging useless. He ducked inside.

The Basement Archives were a tomb.

Stacks of manila folders towered like termite mounds. Metal shelves groaned under decades of secrets – prisoner logs, surveillance authorisations, deportation records, erased coups. The air smelt of mildew, printer ink, and something older – like forgotten time.

Michael moved quickly, guided by the crude map Khalifa had given him. Three aisles in, two rows over. The shelf had been marked with an "X" drawn in biro on masking tape.

But the folder wasn't there.

Only a rectangle of dust where it should've been.

His stomach tightened.

He crouched to scan the lower shelves. Still nothing.

And then – a breath.

Not his own.

He pivoted instinctively, one hand on the butt of his concealed weapon.

Nothing.

Then a whisper. Metal sliding on concrete.

Shit.

He dropped flat as a filing cabinet door clanged above his head. A figure lunged from the shadows – tall, lean, face hidden under a faded army cap and wraparound sunglasses. A local? An enforcer? Too well-trained to be a thug.

Michael rolled, drove a shoulder into the attacker's midsection, and they went crashing through a stack of crates. Papers exploded into the air like bureaucratic confetti.

A blade flashed.

Michael caught the wrist mid-swing and twisted. The knife clattered to the floor. The attacker kneed him hard – ribs. Pain bloomed white. He gasped and headbutted back, catching the man just under the chin.

A moment of disorientation.

Enough.

Michael grabbed the nearest object – an aluminium clipboard – and slammed it down on the attacker's wrist with a sickening crack. The man screamed and staggered back.

Michael didn't hesitate. He landed two solid punches – throat, temple – and the man dropped like a marionette with its strings cut.

Gasping, Michael kicked the blade away, checked the hallway. No footsteps. No alarms.

He turned the attacker over. African. Late 30s. No ID. No phone. Just a stitched symbol inside the jacket collar – an eye inside a triangle. Subtle, but familiar.

Michael pocketed it.

Before leaving, he checked the other shelf compartments. On the bottom rack, tucked behind a broken shredder, he found something – a slim envelope sealed in wax.

No markings. No recipient.

He opened it.

Inside: a single photograph. Grainy. A man bound to a chair. Torture bruises. Face mostly hidden in shadow. But Michael recognised the body type. The tattoo just visible under the sleeve.

Demba.

Alive. At least when the photo was taken.

The envelope also held a key. Small. Rusted. Padlock-style. A tag attached:

BLOCK 5 – CAGE 12

Michael exhaled slowly.

It wasn't over.

Not even close.

Back on the surface, the Ministry had come alive. Staff scurried like ants disturbed. Phones rang. Doors slammed. Something had shifted in the air.

Michael exited the same way he'd entered – calmly, invisibly.

Once outside, he turned down a side street near Congo Cross, ditching the fake badge in a drain and pulling up his collar. His ribs ached. His knuckles were bloodied. But his mind was sharper than it had been in days.

Whoever had attacked him wasn't freelance.

That was a trained operator. Controlled, silent, fast.

And the symbol on the collar – the triangle with the eye – he'd seen it before. Years ago, during a training mission in Ghana. Western contractors. Off-books. Unaccountable. Ghost security. They weren't local.

They were external.

That made this bigger.

Too big to back out now.

Michael's phone vibrated. The burner. He stepped into a recessed doorway and checked it.

One new message.

Coordinates.

No name. No context.

But the location: a warehouse in Cline Town. Not far from the port. Near the old quarantine station.

It could be a trap.

But something told him it wasn't.

It was the next step.

The next brick in Demba's trail.

Michael looked up at the thickening clouds. Rain was coming again.

He welcomed it.

He turned and walked east.

The rain returned in earnest by the time Michael reached Cline Town. It came in sheets, slicing sideways through rusted fences and bouncing off corrugated rooftops like automatic gunfire. Freetown's old industrial quarter was a graveyard of forgotten infrastructure – skeletal cranes, derelict depots, and concrete walls blistered by salt and secrets.

The coordinates led him to an old warehouse near the edge of the port. The kind of place where ships once offloaded bananas and guns in equal measure.

He paused at the chained front gate. Padlock gone. Left swinging.

That was the first sign.

The second was the silence.

No birds. No dogs. Just the soft growl of the Atlantic chewing on the dock pilings beyond the fence.

Michael pushed the gate open and moved in.

The warehouse loomed ahead – two storeys of moss-covered steel and broken glass. Someone had tried to burn it down at some point, but failed. Blackened scorch marks licked the outer walls, but the skeleton held.

He entered through a side door already ajar.

Inside was darkness.

Not the pitch black of night, but the shadowed gloom of places the sun no longer touched. What little light filtered through broken skylights lit up dust motes and exposed broken pallets, mouldy sacks, and coiled ropes.

In the centre of the space was a single plastic chair.

And on the chair – a mobile phone, face down, screen dark. Burner model. Same as his.

Michael approached slowly. Each footstep echoed like a gunshot.

He crouched, turned the phone over.

The screen lit up with a single video file.

PLAY ME.

He scanned the room again. No movement. No sound. But his instincts screamed otherwise. He pressed play.

The screen showed static for a moment. Then a low-resolution video. Demba – unmistakable – hunched in the same chair, but days earlier. A bloodied temple. Split lip. Eyes swollen but defiant.

A voice from offscreen asked: "Who have you told?"

Demba said nothing.

A gloved hand entered the frame, gripped Demba's chin.

"I said – who have you told?"

Demba spat blood. "Everyone. And no one."

The screen cut to black.

Michael swallowed. The timestamp was just four days old.

The screen flashed one final message:

BLOCK 5. STILL ALIVE. FOLLOW THE MARK.

Then the phone died.

Michael stood, alert. His heartbeat thumped in his ears.

Then–

A sound behind him. Not footsteps. Fabric.

He spun.

A woman stood near the entrance. Drenched. Hood pulled back to reveal a high ponytail, face streaked with rain. Eurasian, late thirties. Scar across her right cheek. Military poise. Civilian clothes.

"You're Michael Sillah," she said.

"And you are?"

"Call me Zee."

"No last name?"

"Not one you'd believe."

She stepped closer. No visible weapons, but she moved like she knew how to kill a man in three moves or less.

"Did you leave the phone?" Michael asked.

She ignored it. "They'll be here soon. You have two minutes. Three if they're arguing."

"Who?"

"People who don't like loose ends."

Michael narrowed his eyes. "Who are you working for?"

"I'm working with you," she replied.

He almost laughed. "Forgive me if I find that hard to believe."

She pulled something from her jacket – a sealed envelope. Tossed it onto the chair where the phone had been.

"Proof Demba's alive. Proof someone in the President's office is helping cover it up."

He didn't pick it up. "And what's your angle?"

"I'm one of the loose ends," she said. "I helped smuggle him out of Lungi when they tried to kill him the first time. Now they want us both gone."

Michael stared at her. "Why me?"

"Because you're the only bastard in this country stupid enough to ask the right questions."

From outside – tyres on gravel.

Zee didn't flinch. "It's time."

Michael grabbed the envelope, stuffed it into his coat.

"What now?"

"There's a safehouse in Hill Station. Take Congo Cross, up Spur Road. Red gate with a broken lion."

"You?"

She shook her head. "Different route. We'll regroup after midnight."

"And if I don't come?"

She gave him a look that didn't blink. "You will."

Then she was gone – out through the rear door like smoke.

Michael turned back to the shadows. The chair. The phone. The message. Still alive. Follow the mark.

He scanned the floor again. Something glinted near one of the support pillars. He knelt and picked it up – a cufflink. Gold. Engraved with the initials J.K.

Not Demba's. But familiar.

He pocketed it.

More tyres. Closer now.

A door slammed outside. Then another. Boots on gravel.

Michael moved.

He slipped through the side exit, back into the rain, keeping low. Over the fence. Into the alley behind a line of shipping containers. He crouched behind a stack of oil drums and watched.

Three black SUVs glided into the compound with the silent menace of predators closing in. Armed men poured out. Mismatched gear – some military, some police, some neither. No insignias. No mercy.

They moved fast. Efficient.

Not here for a search.

Here for a kill.

Michael ghosted into the darkness, using the downpour as cover.

He didn't run blindly. He moved with purpose. Left, then hard right, through the old port maze – past cold storage units and empty shipping offices long since gutted by scavengers. He knew this part of the city. The old British colonial grid had never changed. He had used it once to escape a different kind of enemy, during the war.

He ducked into a collapsing tin-roofed shack, caught his breath.

His hands were shaking now. Not from fear – from focus. The edge was back. The hum in his nerves. The electricity that had once made him a hunter of men.

He opened the envelope with a knife.

Inside – photos. Satellite stills. A map of a location marked "BLOCK 5." Not a prison. Not a government site. Something private. Hidden in the hills outside Freetown. A name scrawled in biro on the back of one of the photos: Cyntek Foundation.

Michael stared at it.

He knew the name.

A whisper in meetings. An NGO no one had ever heard of – but always got through checkpoints. Always had a diplomatic tag.

Then, a final item: a matchbook.

One he recognised instantly.

Black velvet cover. Gold foil logo.

Le Sirène.

Freetown's most discreet casino. And the most corrupt.

Michael exhaled, closed the envelope, and slipped it back into his coat.

One thing was certain now.

He was in.

Way in.

The rain had stopped, but Freetown's streets still shimmered in the afterglow. Neon signs bled into puddles. Market stalls had packed up, leaving behind scraps of sugarcane, crushed bottles, and the sweet tang of diesel. Michael's motorbike cut through the night, engine humming low, its light throwing long shadows of things that didn't move.

Le Sirène sat on a crumbling colonial bluff overlooking the ocean. From a distance, it looked like a palace – three storeys of whitewashed ambition with emerald-green shutters and a courtyard strung with fairy lights. Up close, it reeked of power, debt, and secrets. A casino for the elite, the damned, and those who didn't care about the difference.

Michael handed the bike to a valet with a shaved head and dead eyes. No questions. No tickets. Just a nod. The place ran on favours and fear.

Inside, Le Sirène glowed. Marble floors polished like lies. Baccarat tables where warlords and oil barons played with the currency of nations. Champagne bottles lined up like artillery. The air was thick with perfume, gun oil, and bluff.

He kept his pace measured, eyes scanning.

"Mr Sillah," said a voice at his shoulder. "Or are we using another name tonight?"

He turned. Fatima Jalloh. Head of security. Once a tactical police commander. Twice decorated, once betrayed. Her scarlet suit clung like purpose. A Glock tucked discreetly beneath her blazer. She smiled like a cat who'd already eaten.

"I was hoping you'd still be here," he said.

"You don't call, you don't write. The usual."

They walked through the crowd. She waved off a server offering Dom Pérignon like it was tap water. She led him past the blackjack tables, down a corridor lined with oil paintings – the kind looted from other people's empires – and into a private room with mirrored walls and a mahogany table set for two.

"Who told you I was coming?" Michael asked.

"I have ears, and you make noise. Even when you try not to."

She poured herself a finger of whisky – Irish, with the "e" – and left him nothing.

"You're being watched," she said.

"I always am."

"No. I mean in here. They think you're back for something."

"I am."

She raised an eyebrow.

"I need a name," he said. "Someone playing both sides. Maybe someone at Cyntek."

"Everyone at Cyntek is playing both sides," she said, sipping. "That's the business model."

He leaned forward.

"There's a new shipment coming. Medical equipment, according to customs. But Zee tracked the manifest. It's off-books. Headed north, past Makeni. To a place that doesn't exist."

Fatima didn't blink. "Then you already know."

"I want confirmation. I want access."

She considered him for a long moment, eyes flicking to the mirrored wall. "You're still good at getting yourself into places. Less good at getting out."

He shrugged. "Story of my life."

She walked to the wall, pressed a hidden switch. The mirror slid open, revealing a darkened surveillance room. Monitors flickered. One showed the gaming floor. Another, the alley behind the kitchen. A third, zoomed in on Michael's motorbike.

"They tagged your ride," she said.

"Who's watching?"

"Consortium," she said. "Not the one you think. This one's smaller. Meaner. New money. Trying to muscle in."

"What do they want?"

"You. Or to make an example of you."

He exhaled. "Better they try."

A beat passed.

She turned to face him. "You didn't hear this from me. But there's a man – calls himself Pastor. He runs prayer tents in the east. But his name shows up on shipping manifests. And private airstrips."

"Gunrunner?"

"Something worse. Believer."

Michael stood and crossed to the window. Down below, the courtyard buzzed with motion and wealth. Uniformed staff moved like clockwork. A white SUV with tinted windows idled near the service entrance.

"You know this Pastor?" he asked, eyes narrowing.

"We've crossed paths. Never twice in the same skin."

"What's that supposed to mean?"

"He changes names like shirts. And always smells like incense and plastic explosives."

Michael turned. "Where do I find him?"

"He finds you," she said. "He likes theatrics. You'll know when it starts."

The mirror slid shut.

Just then, the door burst open.

Two men. Black suits. No facial expression. Identical. Not brothers. Professionals.

Michael didn't wait.

He threw the whisky glass, shattering it into one man's face. The second reached for his jacket – too slow. Michael closed the gap, elbow to throat, then a knee to the gut. The man folded.

The first lunged, blood in his eye. Michael sidestepped, grabbed his arm, and twisted until the wrist snapped with a crack like a pistol shot.

Fatima had drawn her Glock. She didn't need to use it.

"Still got it," she said.

Michael adjusted his collar, breathing heavy.

"Tell your boss I don't like being tested."

She nodded. "He'll be pleased you passed."

Michael didn't wait to ask.

He left through the kitchen, out the back into the night. Rain threatened again. The air was restless.

So was he.

At the edge of the car park, a figure watched from the shadows, holding a phone to his ear. A single word slipped into the humid night.

"He's active."

Back on the motorbike, Michael peeled off into the darkness, not heading home. He wasn't sure where home was anymore. Only that something was coming.

And whatever it was, it had his name written on it in blood, not ink.

Michael crouched behind a broken concrete wall on the outskirts of Leicester Peak, the glow of Freetown flickering below like a dying constellation. The air was cooler up here. Thinner. But it carried sounds more sharply – the crunch of boots, the rattle of rifles, the distant pulse of drums.

He was off-grid again. The burner phone lay in pieces. No calls. No signals. Just instincts, honed by decades of betrayal and survival.

The safehouse was a ruin – a UN outpost from the 90s, abandoned after the peacekeepers pulled out. Bullet holes pockmarked the walls. Mould crept like ivy. But it had a clear view of the only road up the mountain. And that was enough.

He poured water from his canteen into a cracked mug, then splashed it over his face. The cold bite cleared the residue of adrenaline.

From the shadows, a figure emerged.

Tall, broad, wearing a faded US Army field jacket. Skin like mahogany. Eyes that had seen hell and taken notes.

"Jonas Kamara," Michael said, standing slowly. "I thought you were dead."

"Not yet," Jonas replied, voice a rasp. "But I've been close enough to see what comes after."

They embraced like men who had once pulled each other from burning trucks.

Jonas had been a militia commander in the war – then a fixer for the UN, then a ghost. He only appeared when the stakes were unspeakable.

"I heard you were asking about the Pastor," Jonas said.

Michael nodded. "He's not a preacher."

"No," Jonas said, squatting near the small fire Michael had coaxed into life. "He's a recruiter. Not for God – for chaos."

Jonas threw a folder onto the table. It was bound in twine, stained with something dark.

Inside: satellite images, manifests, intercepted radio chatter.

"He's building something," Jonas continued. "Out near Bonthe. A compound. Guarded by ex-combatants and foreign contractors. He pays in crypto, trades in arms and ideology. And he's got protection – not local. Something more… institutional."

Michael flipped through the images. One caught his eye: a shipping container being offloaded at a jungle clearing. Cyrillic markings. Russian.

"Wagner?" he asked.

"Or a splinter. There's too much happening in the shadows to know for sure."

Michael exhaled.

"What's the endgame?" he asked.

Jonas gave him a look.

"You're standing in it."

A silence stretched between them. Somewhere in the forest, something howled.

Then – a faint hum.

Drones.

Jonas was on his feet instantly.

"They found us."

Michael grabbed his bag, his weapon, his nerve.

They bolted from the outpost, down a narrow trail carved years ago by smugglers. The underbrush clawed at them. The whir of rotors grew louder. Red dots danced on the trees around them.

"Left!" Jonas shouted.

They skidded down a ravine, landing hard. Mud clung to Michael's boots as he scrambled forward.

Behind them, an explosion tore through the ruins of the safehouse. Concrete rained down like shrapnel. The sky lit up.

They didn't stop until they reached the river – dark, swollen, and full of secrets.

They crossed by a fallen tree, slick with moss. On the other side, Jonas collapsed.

"You go," he said between ragged breaths. "They weren't after me."

Michael crouched beside him. "I don't leave allies behind."

Jonas grunted. "Then don't get yourself killed."

Michael hesitated, then handed him a blade.

"Next time," he said, "stab first."

He vanished into the trees.

Dawn broke like a wound over the Atlantic.

Michael reached a village where the roads were still dirt and the shops opened with prayers. He found a public payphone – one of the few still functioning – and fed in enough coins to call a number he hadn't dialled in years.

Three rings. Then a mechanical voice.

"Do you have the number of the beast?"

Michael replied, "It's been disconnected."

A pause.

Then a new voice, clipped, British, female.

"Go to Kenema. Old Catholic mission. Ask for Father Patrick. He's not a priest."

The line went dead.

He hung up and walked away, pulse hammering.

That night, he camped in the bush.

Sleep came slowly. The stars above offered no guidance, just silent witness. He dreamt of a girl with eyes like his – and a voice he hadn't heard in a decade. She stood in the middle of a burning city, whispering something he couldn't make out.

When he woke, his face was wet.

Not with rain.

Tears.

He wiped them away, angry at himself for the weakness, but also for remembering her. Mariama.

Gone.

Forever present.

As the sun rose, Michael stood and slung his bag over his shoulder.

Kenema awaited.

So did Father Patrick – whoever he really was.

And somewhere beyond that, The Pastor.

He wasn't running anymore.

He was hunting.

Michael moved cautiously through the undergrowth, every sense sharpened. The forest whispered in a dozen dialects – birds, insects, the rustle of unseen creatures, the memory of boots where none should be.

He didn't just feel watched. He knew he was.

At the edge of a dried creek bed, he paused. Half-buried in the sand was a torn scrap of fabric – jungle camouflage. Recent. Nearby, a half-smoked cigarette smouldered gently in a puddle.

He wasn't the only one running.

Or hunting.

The next village was ten klicks away, no roads, no signage. Just muscle memory and the map he carried in his head. He'd learned the terrain years ago, during a community policing initiative that turned into something more covert when it became clear cocaine was being trafficked through the forest trails by rebel remnants and ex-mercs.

He reached a clearing by dusk, where the remnants of a schoolhouse stood. Charred beams. A blackboard, still bearing chalked letters in Mende. He stopped and looked around.

Bullet casings.

Recent ones.

He squatted, fingers brushing the brass.

7.62mm NATO.

These weren't rebel weapons.

Whoever had come through here was well-funded, well-supplied. And not local.

Michael stood and scanned the tree line. A flicker of movement – gone. The forest swallowed everything eventually.

But he'd seen enough.

The Pastor wasn't building a cult.

He was building an army.

Michael adjusted his pack and walked on.

Each step forward now was warpath.

CHAPTER 4

A MISSION WITHOUT SAINTS

"When the music changes, so does the dance."
– AFRICAN PROVERB

The road to Kenema was a battered ribbon of cracked asphalt and red dust, twisting through the rainforest like a forgotten artery. The Land Cruiser bucked over potholes deep enough to swallow cattle, the suspension groaning in protest as Michael watched the treeline blur past. Diesel, wet earth, overripe mangoes – the scent of the interior hung thick in the warm air pouring through the half-open window.

The driver hadn't spoken since Bo. Whether by choice or instruction didn't matter. Jonas had arranged him – paid in cash and favours, the quiet kind that never made it into ledgers. A tap of the map, a single nod, and silence had taken the front seat.

Villages slid by: half-built homes of mud and tin; churches with bullet holes in their roofs; barefoot children waving with hands open to the world and eyes closed to its dangers. Then the forest thickened, swallowing the signs of habitation until the only markers were the shifting shapes of great silk-cotton trees and the occasional glint of a river snaking between the undergrowth.

Kenema loomed ahead as the late afternoon light faded into amber. Always wilder than Freetown – more frontier than capital – but now the air carried tension. Military trucks moved in pairs. Men in plain clothes stood too still at corners. Even the breeze seemed to hesitate before crossing the street.

The Land Cruiser rolled to a stop outside the Old Catholic Mission – a whitewashed compound with rusting iron gates and walls tall enough to suggest sanctuary, or imprisonment. From outside it looked abandoned. But the neglect was a disguise, and not a convincing one.

Michael stepped out. The engine was already fading into the distance.

Then the gate creaked open on its own.

The courtyard inside was overgrown, the bell tower crumbling, statues of saints stripped of their faces by weather and neglect. But the silence wasn't empty – it thrumed, like the pause before rain breaks open the sky.

He stepped into the chapel.

A man sat alone in the front pew – white cassock, trimmed beard, dark skin. Eyes like obsidian, too still to belong to a man of God.

"Father Patrick," Michael said. His voice echoed in the cavernous room.

The man didn't turn. "That name's for the locals. For you, Michael, let's keep it simpler – call me what I used to be: Patrick O'Kane."

Michael blinked. "MI6?"

A faint smile. "Once. These days I answer to different masters."

Patrick rose and walked to the altar, lighting a single candle. "Still say Mass sometimes. Faith keeps the villagers grounded. Even if the clergy can't."

"Is that why I'm here? Grounding?"

"No," Patrick said. "You're here because something's coming, and the people pulling the strings don't like surprises."

Michael took a seat. "The Pastor?"

That made Patrick pause. "You've seen him?"

"Not directly. But I've seen what he's building. Contractors. Weapons. A compound near Bonthe. Someone's funding him."

Patrick exhaled slowly. "Then you're already ahead of most."

He unlocked a cabinet behind the altar and withdrew a thick file – redacted pages, satellite images, shipping manifests. He handed it over. "MI6 has eyes on him, but not hands. He's useful to certain people. Until he's not."

Michael leafed through: images of the compound, a shipment from Odessa, a blurred figure with head bowed and face obscured.

"What's his real name?"

"Doesn't matter," Patrick said. "What matters is who protects him."

"The Consortium?"

"They don't protect. They exploit. He's a spark plug they can drop into any unstable engine."

Michael considered that. "Why help me?"

"Because I've seen what happens when people like you go in blind."

"People like me?"

Patrick's expression darkened. "Men who still believe doing good means doing right. That honour exists. That justice is real. That sort of idealism gets people killed."

Michael didn't flinch. "Then why call me?"

Patrick looked away. "Because your conviction makes you dangerous. And maybe that makes you useful."

A tall nun appeared in the doorway, silent and shrouded.

"She'll take you to your room," Patrick said. "You leave at dawn."

"To where?"

Patrick held his gaze. "To the edge of something that doesn't yet have a name."

His room was spartan – bed, basin, barred window. A crucifix hung above the headboard like a sentinel. The walls were thick and soundproofed. The file Patrick had given him lay open on the bedspread, its pages less like intelligence and more like invitations to war.

The final page was hand-drawn: coordinates, a red X, and beneath it, in Patrick's handwriting:

Trust no one. Not even me.

Michael tried to sleep. Rest came in fragments, never deep enough to quiet the noise in his head. Every sound outside – a shifting branch, a distant engine, the hum of insects – yanked him back to the surface.

A soft knock. Two taps. Silence.

Michael was upright immediately.

He slid the knife from under his pillow and approached the door.

The nun stood in the hallway, holding a tray with tea and a folded note.

"No one comes here at night," she said softly. "Not without purpose."

Michael took the note. The handwriting was unfamiliar – sharper, rushed.

The Pastor meets with foreign buyers. Port of Sulima. Midnight.

Do not trust the Father. He is not what he pretends to be.

No signature.

When he looked up again, the nun was already gone.

Michael shut the door and read the note a second, then a third time.

Someone inside the mission was playing both sides.

Or all sides.

And dawn suddenly felt very far away.

Michael left the Old Catholic Mission before dawn, the mist hanging low over the compound like breath on glass. The air was cool, the quiet deceptive. He carried no luggage – only a shoulder bag with the burner phone, the red dossier, and the warning note that gnawed at the back of his mind.

A battered Hilux waited beyond the gates. The woman behind the wheel didn't smile.

"Kadiatu," she said before he could ask. Her voice was brisk, practical. "You owe Jonas for this lift. I don't like detours."

"I'm not here for friendship," Michael replied, climbing in.

She shifted into gear, tyres spitting gravel. "Good. I don't have time for that either."

The road south unfolded like a promise never meant to be kept. Red earth washed clean by rain. Palms leaning conspiratorially over the track. The jungle pressed in from both sides as if trying to erase the way forward. They followed the twisting course of the Moa River, its dark sheen occasionally visible through gaps in the foliage.

Kadiatu drove like a woman who knew every hidden checkpoint, every place the trees concealed men with rifles. She hummed under her breath to a radio station that came and went in the static. Without looking, she reached into the glovebox and handed Michael a banana and a sachet of water.

He accepted both.

"Sulima doesn't like strangers," she said.

"Then we'll fit in nicely."

A rare flicker of amusement crossed her face.

They passed an unofficial roadblock – young men in mismatched uniforms with Kalashnikovs held casually, almost carelessly. Kadiatu barely slowed. She flicked a laminated badge across the dashboard. The guards waved them through without a word.

"Who were they?" Michael asked.

"Local security committee," she said. "Or gang boys with radios. Hard to tell these days."

By the time they reached Sulima, the sun was high and the air heavy with the stench of diesel, fish guts, and brackish water. The town sprawled across the river delta like a memory of prosperity – rusting fishing boats, half-built concrete shells, vendors selling dried catfish beside buckets of illegal fuel.

Children splashed in the shallows. Women stared with the world-weariness of those who'd seen too many men with too many promises.

Kadiatu parked behind a corrugated shack near the docks.

"We walk from here," she said. "Quietly."

They moved through narrow alleys between warehouse walls, avoiding sleeping dogs and men who watched without watching. At the far end of the dock, under a sagging tarpaulin, a crane was offloading a container from a grey, unmarked cargo ship.

Michael lifted his phone and zoomed in.

MUNITIONS – GRADE B

Origin: Turkiye

Receiver: The Gideon Foundation

His stomach tightened.

The Gideon Foundation – the Pastor's humanitarian façade. Bible verses on their website, food packages for photos, and offshore accounts filled with blood money. The perfect mask for a man who traded faith for firepower.

A forklift moved the crate onto a flatbed truck. Six armed men stood around it – matching boots, clean rifles. Professionals.

"You getting all this?" Kadiatu whispered.

Michael nodded.

"We can't stop it," she said.

"We don't need to," he replied. "Not yet."

They slipped away through the back of a fish market, the air buzzing with flies and thick with rot and bleach.

As they approached the Hilux, Michael slowed. Something was wrong – an old tingle of instinct prickling beneath his skin.

A man stood beside the pickup.

Charcoal trench coat. Dead eyes. A cigarette glowing faintly in the dawn light.

The Fixer.

Kadiatu tensed. "You know him?"

Michael nodded once. "Too well."

The Fixer didn't move. Didn't speak. Just watched them with the stillness of a predator that had already chosen the moment of the kill. He exhaled a plume of smoke, turned, and walked away – slow, deliberate, like punctuation at the end of a threat.

"That's a message," Kadiatu muttered.

"Yeah," Michael said quietly. "That I'm not as off-grid as I thought."

They drove in silence. Michael's mind was a tangle of shifting intel, instinct, and unease. The jungle peeled back in flashes of green as the Hilux rattled north.

After a long silence, Kadiatu spoke. "You didn't tell me we were being followed."

"I didn't know."

"That's worse."

"I'll fix it."

"You'd better."

She adjusted her grip on the wheel. "What's your stake in all this?"

He didn't answer immediately. "And yours?"

"I don't like what the Pastor's building. Too many foreigners. Too much money. Too many rumours about disappearances." She paused. "This isn't religion. This is preparation."

"Preparation for what?"

"That's what scares me," she said. "No one knows."

They hit a pothole hard enough to jolt her back in her seat.

"Where to now?" she asked.

Michael stared straight ahead, the road narrowing as if funneling them toward something inevitable.

"I need to see Patrick again," he said. "This time, I want straight answers."

By the time Michael returned to the mission compound, night had settled over Kenema like a velvet shroud. The power was out again. A single candle flickered on the veranda, its glow snatching at shadows that clung to the courtyard walls.

Patrick was waiting.

Barefoot in a wooden chair, sleeves rolled, his white linen shirt faintly stained with palm oil and the sweat of a long day. He looked like a man who'd seen too much and slept too little – which, Michael suspected, wasn't far from the truth.

Michael stepped into the circle of light.

"We need to talk," he said.

Patrick gestured toward the spare chair and poured himself a measure of Johnnie Walker Red. "I wondered how long it would take you to come back angry."

Michael remained standing. "We were burned. At Sulima."

A flicker crossed Patrick's face. Concern? Guilt? Calculation? It was gone too fast to read.

"Define burned."

"The Fixer was there," Michael said. "Before we left. Just stood there watching."

Patrick exhaled slowly. "Did he follow you?"

"No. He didn't need to."

Their eyes locked, and something old and jagged slid between them like a memory neither wanted to touch.

"You think I sold you out," Patrick said quietly.

"I think someone did," Michael replied. "And only three people knew where I was going."

"That's a heavy accusation."

"It's not an accusation," Michael said. "Not yet."

Silence. Thick. Scarred.

Patrick looked toward the distant ridge where the faint lights of Kenema flickered like dying stars. "Do you remember Cotonou?"

Michael's jaw tightened. "Barely got out alive."

Patrick nodded. "And we did. Because we trusted each other. Because neither of us blinked."

Michael took one deliberate step forward. "This isn't Cotonou. This thing with the Pastor – it's different. It's layered."

Patrick rubbed his temples, the candlelight casting long shadows across his face. "You're not wrong. But you're playing checkers on a chessboard that's been rigged since the first move."

"Then level with me."

Patrick hesitated – just for a heartbeat. A hairline crack in his composure. Then he rose and disappeared into a back room, returning with a black folder wrapped in duct tape.

He dropped it on the table.

"The Black File."

Michael stared. "I thought that was a rumour."

"It was," Patrick said. "Until Jonas got hold of a partial copy. Three people died getting this out."

Michael peeled away the tape. Inside was a mosaic of horror:

- Satellite images
- Banking flows
- Redacted embassy cables
- Contractor manifests
- Russian, French, and English stamps overlapping like fingerprints

At the centre of it all:

The Gideon Foundation.

The Pastor.

Foreign military contractors across West Africa.

Psychological operations.

Arms routes. Training camps. Cuts of election funding.

Not chaos.

Design.

"This isn't proxy conflict," Michael said quietly. "This is structural destabilisation."

Patrick tapped the folder. "They don't just want influence. They want leverage. National leverage. Security leverage. Narrative leverage."

"And you sat on this?" Michael asked.

"I was verifying it."

Michael took a step away, pacing. "You should've brought this to me the moment it crossed your desk."

"And what would you have done?" Patrick asked. "Gone rogue in the jungle? Exposed it before we knew who to trust? You've seen what happens when we move too soon."

Michael stopped, his silhouette framed by the candlelight. "We're already too late."

Patrick poured a second drink and pushed it across the table – a peace offering neither intended to accept.

"You need to contact London," Patrick said. "Not the official channels. The backdoor."

Michael hesitated. "He said not to involve them yet."

"Then he was wrong," Patrick replied. "Or he's out of time."

Reluctantly, Michael pulled out the burner phone. Entered a secure sequence.

Two rings. A click.

A clipped British voice answered. "Zero?"

Michael replied: "Redhawk. Compromised. Requisitioning escalation file."

A pause. "Confirmed. Upload Black File extract to Node Three. Burn the original. Stand by for instruction set. No further direct comms."

The line went dead.

Patrick raised his glass. "Well. We're in it now."

Michael didn't smile. "We always were."

He was about to speak again when a rustle broke across the compound. Quick, sharp. Wrong.

Patrick's eyes narrowed. "That wasn't one person. Three. Running."

They moved fast – Michael sweeping low across the courtyard, Patrick circling wide with silent precision.

Another rustle. A muffled gasp.

Michael reached the gate and yanked it open.

Kadiatu staggered inside, blood smeared down her arm, breath ragged.

"Jonas is gone," she gasped. "They got to him."

Michael felt something twist deep in his chest. "Gone how?"

"Not dead," she said. "Taken. Moving fast. Sulima was just the opening act."

Patrick joined them, expression darkening. "We need to disappear. Regroup."

"No," Michael said. "We go after Jonas."

"That's suicide," Patrick replied.

Michael's eyes hardened. "It's justice."

Kadiatu winced, pressing her side. "They weren't amateurs. This was military kit. Radio chatter. Drones."

Michael's heartbeat skipped. "Drones?"

"Fixed-wing," she said. "High altitude. Someone's giving them ISR support."

Patrick swore under his breath. "That means state-level backing."

Michael scanned the Black File again. Red lines connecting dots across continents. Too many foreign seals. Too many shadows.

"Then we hit their logistics," he said. "Break their chain. We don't need to win – we just need to crack this thing open."

Patrick looked at Kadiatu. "Do you know where they're holding him?"

She nodded weakly. "A farm near Waterloo. Remote. No signal. Used to be a cocoa operation."

Michael holstered his pistol. "Then that's where we start."

The candle flickered.

No more shadows to hide in.

No more illusions of safety.

Just the road – and whatever waited at the end of it.

The road to Waterloo was barely a road at all – just a gouged-out trail of red laterite twisting through jungle that swallowed the headlights whole. Michael drove with lights off, the faint half-moon barely enough to catch fallen branches and ruts deep enough to snap an axle. The engine grumbled as if protesting the terrain.

Patrick sat beside him, rifle balanced across his knees, his posture taut, scanning the tree line with the twitchy stillness of a man expecting ghosts. Kadiatu – pale beneath the dirt and blood smearing her thigh – sat in the back seat, whispering coded instructions into a scrambled radio.

"No chatter. No names," she murmured. "We're dark from here."

The cocoa farm appeared like an apparition between the trees – a cluster of low concrete buildings huddled around a central yard, the silhouette of a collapsed drying shed stabbing toward the sky like broken ribs. No movement. No floodlights. No guards visible.

Too quiet.

Michael cut the engine.

"This is it," he said.

They fanned out silently into the humid dark – Kadiatu limping around the northern perimeter, Patrick slipping left like a shadow cut from the night, while Michael moved straight and low toward the barn. The moon slid behind cloud. The world shrank to breath, heartbeat, and the faint crunch of soil under boots.

Michael reached the barn first. A dim light flickered behind its wooden slats – unstable, as though struggling to stay alive.

Then he heard it.

A cough. Human. Weak.

He edged forward, weapon raised.

Inside, Jonas sat tied to a rusted metal chair, his face swollen and broken, blood dried across his shirt, a harsh spotlight angled up into his eyes. The shadows behind the beam swallowed everything else.

Michael stepped inside.

That's when the night exploded.

Gunfire erupted from the treeline – short, sharp, suppressed bursts slicing through the dark. Patrick's voice crackled over the comms:

"Contact left! Two shooters – military rig!"

Michael ducked as a round punched through the barn wall an inch from his head, splinters grazing his cheek. He dropped to one knee and returned fire – two quick controlled shots. A shadow folded with a groan.

"Jonas!" he shouted. "Can you move?"

Jonas winced. "Cut me loose… they're not alone."

Michael sliced the ropes with a knife and hauled him upright. Another burst tore through a stack of cocoa sacks.

Outside, Kadiatu's voice cut in:

"One down! Second moving northeast – fast!"

Then a new sound drifted across the compound – a high, fast buzz. Insectile. Predatory.

Michael's blood turned to ice.

A drone.

He looked up through a gap in the roof and caught the faint sweep of a green targeting laser painting the yard.

"They're marking targets!" he snapped. "Patrick – eyes up! ISR asset overhead!"

"I see it," Patrick replied. "Fall back to the vehicle – now!"

Michael dragged Jonas behind the ruined generator at the rear of the barn. Another shooter broke from the treeline – tactical vest, NVGs, suppressed rifle. A professional.

Michael fired once. Clean. Centre mass.

The man went down like a puppet whose strings had been cut.

As the mercenary collapsed, something primal surged inside Michael – cold, hard, focused. Not rage. Not revenge.

Necessity.

And it stayed with him.

They scrambled back toward the hidden vehicle. Patrick was already there, engine turning over, headlights still dark. Kadiatu emerged from the trees limping heavily, blood streaming down her thigh.

"You hit?" Michael asked.

"Through and through," she muttered. "Didn't touch bone. But it'll need whisky and stitches."

Gunfire chased them as they sped into the forest, the branches whipping against the sides of the vehicle like grasping hands.

Ten minutes later, the jungle swallowed the sounds of pursuit.

Static crackled across Kadiatu's radio as the scrambled line reconnected.

Jonas coughed blood. "They moved the Pastor," he rasped. "A week ago. This was a trap. They left me as bait."

Michael frowned. "Who moved him?"

Jonas swallowed painfully. "Didn't say. Just one word… 'Umbra.'"

Patrick stiffened beside him.

Michael caught it immediately. "You know that name?"

"Not a name," Patrick said quietly. "A designation. Tier-1 clearance."

Kadiatu leaned forward. "Tier-1 of who?"

Patrick hesitated, jaw tightening. "It means off-book. Beyond standard authorisation."

"Off whose book?" she pressed.

Patrick didn't answer. He didn't need to. The silence said everything.

Michael pulled the vehicle into a concealed clearing, killed the engine, and turned back to Jonas. "Anything else?"

Jonas raised a trembling hand and pointed southeast. "The barn… floorboards…"

Michael exchanged a look with Patrick. "We're going back."

Kadiatu swore under her breath. "You're insane."

"No," Michael said. "Thorough."

They doubled back on foot, moving through the undergrowth in complete silence. The drone had moved on, or changed altitude – the sky was clear.

The barn smouldered with the aftershocks of the firefight. Smoke curled lazily up into the trees. Michael slipped inside first, Patrick covering the door with ruthless efficiency.

Jonas was right.

Under a loose board – concealed beneath dried cocoa husk – Michael found a metal crate. Matte black. Humming faintly, like a heartbeat trapped in steel.

He opened it.

Inside were encrypted hard drives, a ruggedised field router, two shortwave transmitters, and–

"Jesus," Patrick whispered.

A tactical map of the region, marked in red.

Not English.

Not French.

Cyrillic.

And on the inside lid, a screen still active – relaying a low-bandwidth satellite uplink bouncing between nodes in:

South Sudan.

Malta.

The Azores.

This wasn't a mercenary outfit.

This was infrastructure.

State-level.

"Someone's building a forward operation," Patrick said numbly. "Mapping. Signals. Intercepts. Movement logs. Possibly prepping for kinetic assets."

Michael felt the chill settle in his spine. "This farm was a node."

Kadiatu hovered over the screen, eyes wide. "Who the hell has the budget for this?"

"Not a cartel," Michael said. "And not warlords."

He closed the crate.

"This is bigger."

Patrick nodded. "Much bigger."

They torched everything – a controlled burn, white flames licking over metal, wires, and plastic until the barn glowed like an open wound in the jungle.

Jonas watched it in silence, his eyes dark and distant.

Then they left.

They drove through the back roads toward Freetown in silence, the early light bleeding slowly into the sky. The jungle thinned. The river mist thickened. The Land Cruiser juddered as it hit a patch of broken tarmac outside Waterloo, the suspension groaning in protest.

Jonas coughed again – a wet, rattling sound that made Kadiatu twist in her seat.

"Easy," she murmured, steadying him as the car bounced. "We've got you."

Patrick kept his eyes on the mirrors. "No drones. No tails. Whoever hit that farm has pulled back. For now."

Michael didn't respond. His jaw was set like stone, his mind running through layers of implication and threat. The Pastor had fled. The mercenaries were too organised. The drone support was too clean. The Black File pointed to something vast, architectural, deliberate.

Umbra.

That single word felt like sand in his teeth.

He glanced at Jonas – pale, sweating, eyes drifting. "Stay awake," Michael said softly. "We're not far."

"Didn't think…" Jonas whispered. "Didn't think… anyone would come."

Michael's voice stayed level. "We don't leave our own behind."

A faint smile cracked Jonas's bloodied lips. "Not… what I heard… about you."

Michael's expression didn't shift, but something moved inside him. A shadow he'd carried for years.

He didn't answer.

They reached a back alley near the safehouse in Freetown – an unmarked compound tucked between a half-finished apartment block and an abandoned workshop. Patrick killed the engine while Kadiatu climbed out, pressing a hand to her wounded leg.

"We need a medic," she muttered.

"We need discretion more," Patrick replied. "No hospitals. We patch up here."

Michael helped Jonas inside, lowering him gently onto a narrow cot in the dimly lit back room. The air smelled of disinfectant and rusted metal.

Kadiatu pulled a med kit from the shelf. "Hold him."

They worked in grim silence – stitching Jonas's shoulder, cleaning the gashes across his ribs, binding cracked cartilage. Jonas winced but didn't cry out.

"You've been through worse," Michael said quietly.

"Not recently," Jonas croaked.

Kadiatu straightened up, wiping sweat from her brow. "He'll heal. Slowly. But he'll heal."

Patrick moved into the doorway, rifle slung over his shoulder. "We need to talk."

Michael followed him outside into the narrow alley. Patrick lit a cigarette, the flame illuminating the weary lines around his eyes.

"That drone wasn't local," Patrick said.

"I know."

"Probably leased. Shallow orbit. Meaning short-range control. Meaning someone nearby was watching that farm in real time."

Michael folded his arms. "Umbra."

Patrick nodded slowly. "Not a codename. A classification. Beyond the normal black-budget operations." He took a drag, exhaled. "This is multinational. Coordinated. The Pastor's just one spoke in the wheel."

Michael watched traffic pass faintly at the end of the alley – poda-podas groaning under their own weight, market hawkers shouting for morning business, the city waking and not knowing how close it had come to a firestorm.

Patrick continued, "You know what this means."

"It means," Michael said, "we aren't just chasing the Pastor anymore. We're chasing whoever controls him."

"And they know we're coming," Patrick said.

Michael looked up at the pale dawn sky. "Let them prepare."

Kadiatu limped out to join them. She tossed something toward Michael. He caught it.

A silver ring.

Etched with a serpent devouring its own tail.

Found in the pocket of the mercenary he'd killed.

Michael turned it in his hand. "This wasn't on any uniform."

"Exactly," Kadiatu said. "These people aren't ghosts. They're architects."

Patrick inhaled sharply. "And they're leaving calling cards."

Michael pocketed the ring. "Then we follow the trail."

A sound drifted from inside – Jonas coughing again. Kadiatu went to him.

Patrick lowered his voice. "There's something else you need to know."

Michael met his eye. "Say it."

"The London backdoor you used last night..." Patrick hesitated. "It was accessed again. From an unknown terminal."

"When?"

"Twenty minutes after you closed the line."

Michael's pulse slowed. Hardened. "Someone's watching us."

"Closer than you think."

Michael didn't blink. "Good. Saves us looking."

Patrick almost smiled – almost. "You're playing with fire."

"I know," Michael said. "But fire's all we have left."

Miles away, deep in the brush near the burned-out farm, a lone figure stood atop a ridge. He wore a charcoal suit, dusty boots, and no insignia. His night-vision binoculars dangled against his chest.

He turned them over in his hands.

A serpent ring glinted on his finger – identical to the one Michael now carried.

He checked his watch. The second hand swept in perfect silence.

He smiled.

"Phase two begins."

He turned toward the forest.

And vanished into it.

CHAPTER 5

SHADOWS ACROSS CONAKRY

"When elephants fight, it is the grass that suffers."
– AFRICAN PROVERB

Dawn crept slowly over Freetown, pale light filtering through the half-broken shutters of the safehouse. Michael sat alone at the table, elbows planted on either side of the battered radio unit, watching the green LED flicker with weak life. The compound still smelt of antiseptic and stale smoke from the night before.

Jonas slept in the back room, patched and breathing steadily thanks to Kadiatu's quick work. Patrick was somewhere on the roof, pretending to keep watch but really avoiding conversation – the man had secrets layered like sediment.

Michael wasn't sure how much more sediment he could tolerate.

He reached into his pocket and turned the silver ring over in his fingers.

A serpent devouring its own tail.

The symbol of Umbra.

Not a name.

Not a codename.

A designation.

The kind given only to operations completely off the books – and as far as Michael could tell, operating beyond any single nation's interest. That frightened him more than any armed convoy or drone strike.

Footsteps sounded in the corridor. Kadiatu stepped into the room, wearing cargo trousers, a faded football shirt, and fresh bandages on her thigh. She moved stiffly, but she moved.

"You should be lying down," Michael said.

She snorted. "And you should be less annoying. Neither of us is getting what we want today."

He allowed the corner of his mouth to twitch. "How's Jonas?"

"Asleep. Stubborn. Alive." She dropped into the chair opposite him. "He's lucky. Those mercenaries weren't questioning him. They were softening him for transit."

"To where?" Michael asked.

"That's what bothers me." She traced a circle on the table with one finger. "People disappear in this region all the time. But Jonas? Someone wanted him intact."

Michael leaned back. "Because of what he stole."

"You mean the Black File?" Kadiatu lowered her voice. "Patrick told me pieces. Not enough."

"Be grateful," Michael said. "Once you know all of it, you stop sleeping."

She studied him for a long moment. "You think Jonas is safe?"

"As safe as anyone is around me."

That earned an eyebrow. "You say that like it's a warning."

"It is."

Patrick entered with the subtlety of a man born to surveillance, every step soft on the cracked tiles.

"We're moving," he said.

Kadiatu straightened. "To where?"

"Conakry," Patrick replied. "We've already been flagged in Sierra Leone. Too many eyes. Too many whispers. Guinea buys us time."

Michael watched him carefully. Patrick was too calm. Too rehearsed.

"What aren't you saying?" Michael asked.

Patrick rolled his shoulders, tension briefly visible. "Umbra's watchers aren't just in-country. London pinged another backdoor attempt this morning. Someone traced our last call. They're triangulating."

Michael set the ring down. "So we're running."

"We're repositioning," Patrick corrected, grabbing a worn canvas bag from the counter. "There's a man in Conakry who can help us disappear long enough to see the board clearly."

"Who?" Michael asked.

"Maxime Touré."

Kadiatu let out a low whistle. "You didn't tell him about Touré?"

Michael shook his head.

Patrick rubbed his forehead. "Touré is… complicated. Former intelligence liaison. Half-French, half-devil. Harvests information like other men harvest rice."

"He trustworthy?" Michael asked.

"No," Patrick said flatly. "But he's useful. And right now, that'll have to do."

They left the safehouse through the rear alley, keeping to the narrow paths that cut between rusting fuel drums and stacks of discarded tyres. Patrick led the way with that precise, economical gait that made him seem half-shadow. Kadiatu brought up the rear, her limp masked well behind steady footing.

Their vehicle – a nondescript Prado with peeling paint – idled quietly behind a row of abandoned workshops. Michael checked the perimeter twice, instincts prickling in the warm morning air.

Something felt off.

Too quiet.

Too neat.

He slid into the passenger seat.

"Drive," Patrick said.

The road to the border was a long, wavering scar that cut through communities still waking. Smoke curled from cookfires, children chased chickens between shacks, women carried buckets of water balanced effortlessly atop their heads. The world looked unchanged – comfortingly ordinary – but Michael knew too much now to take comfort in stillness.

Stillness meant someone was waiting.

They passed Hastings and Waterloo without incident, though Michael noticed two motorcycles trailing them for several minutes before veering off abruptly. Not amateurs – watchers.

Patrick noticed too. He tapped the dashboard once. "Eyes front. Let them peel away."

Kadiatu glanced in the mirror. "Someone's marking us."

"Of course they are," Patrick said. "We aren't invisible. Just harder to track when we keep moving."

They remained silent until the Sierra Leone–Guinea border came into view – a chaotic cluster of makeshift stalls, security booths, and a half-collapsed concrete archway pockmarked by rust and weather.

Patrick handed Michael a forged passport. "You're Michael Conteh today. NGO assessor."

Kadiatu muttered, "You don't look like an NGO assessor."

"That's the point," Patrick said. "Assessors are always stressed, underpaid, and annoyed. You'll fit right in."

For the first time, Michael allowed himself a quiet laugh.

The crossing went smoother than expected – a few questions, some sideways glances, a discreet bribe slid across a counter – and they were through. Guinea stretched out before them, hot, dusty, crowded, and loud.

But Conakry was different.

Conakry held ghosts.

And some of them wore rings.

By the time they reached the outskirts of the city, the sun had climbed high enough to bleach the sky. Conakry spread out along the peninsula like a beast coiled between the Atlantic and its own contradictions – vibrant, chaotic, corruptible, alive.

Traffic swallowed them whole – poda-podas darting like angry insects, yellow taxis weaving between trucks loaded with plantains, goats, and far more people than physics ought to allow.

Patrick leaned back. "Maxime's expecting us."

"That supposed to make me feel better?" Michael asked.

"No. It's supposed to make you cautious."

"Already am."

"Good," Patrick said. "You'll need to be."

They turned down a narrow side road toward Kaloum, the administrative heart – colonial structures decaying under new paint, ministries doubling as storage sheds, policemen napping beneath jacaranda trees.

Patrick nodded at a corner café. "We meet our contact there. A journalist. Trustworthy enough."

Michael snorted. "Your standards are slipping."

"They'd have to, to work with you."

Michael didn't rise to it.

As they parked, the café's door opened.

A woman stepped out – dark, poised, wearing a pale blue headscarf and a gaze sharp enough to cut glass.

Aïcha Diallo.

She moved toward them with cool, deliberate confidence.

"You're late," she said.

Patrick opened his mouth, but she raised a hand. "And don't blame traffic. I checked the cameras."

Kadiatu blinked. "You have access to traffic cameras?"

"I have access," Aïcha said, "to many things."

Her attention shifted to Michael – assessing, measuring.

"So," she said. "You're the one Umbra has been looking for."

Heat tightened behind Michael's ribs.

"How do you know that?" he asked.

Aïcha's expression didn't shift.

"Because," she said quietly, "I've been looking for you as well."

Aïcha turned and walked into the café without waiting. Patrick followed with the air of a man bracing for impact. Kadiatu and Michael exchanged a look – hers suspicious, his calculating – then stepped inside.

The café was dim, lit only by slatted sunlight cutting through dusty blinds. Ceiling fans churned lazily overhead. The smell of strong coffee and stale sugar hung beneath the low murmur of a radio broadcasting highlife music.

Aïcha slid into a booth at the back, the one furthest from the street, with a clear line to both exits. A professional's choice.

"You're not what I expected," she said to Michael as he sat opposite her.

"I get that a lot."

"Hmm." She studied him like someone reading an encrypted document. "Men who've seen what you've seen usually carry it in their eyes. But yours… it's buried deeper."

Michael didn't rise to the bait. "You said you were looking for me."

"I was." She reached into her bag and withdrew a slim envelope. "And not because I enjoy making new friends."

Patrick shifted. "Show him."

Aïcha placed the envelope on the table. Michael opened it.

Inside were three photographs.

All grainy. All taken from height. Drone height.

1. Michael at the Sulima docks.
2. Michael leaving the mission in Kenema.
3. Michael standing over a collapsed mercenary at the cocoa farm.

Each image was stamped with a timecode. Each carried the faint imprint of Cyrillic text in the margins.

Michael exhaled slowly. "Who took these?"

"Umbra," Aïcha said.

Kadiatu frowned. "How did you get them?"

Aïcha tapped her temple. "Contacts. Everywhere. Umbra's operations leak – not often, but enough if you know where to listen."

Patrick crossed his arms. "Umbra doesn't leak. Ever."

"That's what people like Umbra want you to think," Aïcha replied. "No structure is perfect. And no conspiracy is airtight."

Michael placed the photos back on the table. "Why show me this?"

"Because you're in the middle of something you don't understand." Her eyes shifted to Patrick. "And because your friend here has been sitting on too many truths for far too long."

Patrick stiffened. "Careful."

"No," she said. "You be careful."

The tension between them crackled like static.

Aïcha turned back to Michael. "You want answers. Good. I want something too."

Michael raised an eyebrow. "Which is?"

"Keita," she said simply.

Kadiatu blinked. "The analyst from Lungi?"

Aïcha nodded. "He's missing."

Patrick swore under his breath.

"He didn't defect," Aïcha continued. "He didn't run. He was taken. And before he disappeared, he sent one encrypted message to my desk."

She slid a folded piece of paper across the table.

Michael opened it.

On it was a single word:

UMBRA

And beneath it, an eight-digit code.

"Coordinates?" Michael asked.

"No," said Aïcha. "A dead-drop reference. One used only by people in deep-cover intelligence roles. Keita knew he was compromised. He used this to point me to his last movements."

"And you want us to find him?" Michael asked.

"I want you to help me decode the network that kidnapped him." Her tone cooled. "Keita wasn't just an analyst. He was my partner. And Umbra made it personal."

The table fell silent.

Finally Michael spoke. "Where do we start?"

Aïcha nodded toward the window. "With Maxime Touré."

Patrick groaned softly. "Of course."

"He's already expecting you," she continued. "And before you ask – yes, he knows more than he ever says. Yes, you can trust him… to a point. And no, he will not like you."

"Why not?" Michael asked.

Aïcha's lips curved slightly. "Because Maxime doesn't like anyone who reminds him of himself."

They left the café through the back entrance, emerging into a side street where vendors sold pirated DVDs, plastic combs, and SIM cards from faded cardboard stalls. The sea breeze carried the smell of brine and diesel from the port.

Patrick led them down a narrow alley. "Maxime operates out of Coyah these days. Keeps a small estate. Surrounded by enough muscle to invade a small country."

"And we're just walking in?" Kadiatu asked.

"No," Patrick replied. "We're being invited."

"That better be true," she muttered.

Traffic thickened as they left Kaloum and merged into the mainland sprawl. Market stalls spilled onto the road. Goats darted between engines. A boy no older than ten tried to sell them cold water bags through the window.

Despite the noise, Michael felt the quiet pressure of being followed – unmarked vehicles shadowing them in the distance, motorbikes slipping into view at odd intervals.

Not close enough to confront.

But close enough to watch.

"Aïcha was right," he murmured.

Patrick grunted. "Umbra rarely loses sight of people they mark."

"And they've marked us," Michael said.

"Oh," Patrick replied, "they marked you long before Sierra Leone."

Michael looked at him sharply. "Meaning?"

Patrick kept his gaze on the road. "Meaning Umbra doesn't chase men who stumble into their path. They chase men who can threaten it."

Michael absorbed that in silence.

They turned onto the highway toward Coyah a long stretch of asphalt flanked by sugarcane fields and half-built structures abandoned before paint could touch cement. The wind carried heat waves strong enough to blur the horizon.

"Maxime's place is beyond the toll," Patrick said. "High walls. Two guard posts. Don't speak unless spoken to."

Kadiatu smirked. "Sounds like home."

Michael checked the ring in his pocket again – the serpent devouring its own tail. Somehow heavier than before.

"Patrick," he said quietly, "does Maxime know about Umbra?"

Patrick hesitated. A tiny flicker. But enough.

"He knows pieces," Patrick answered. "More than most. Less than he thinks. Enough to be dangerous."

"To whom?" Michael asked.

Patrick didn't answer.

Because they were already pulling up to the gates.

Tall. Reinforced. Painted black.

And guarded by two men who looked like they'd been forged rather than born.

As the gates opened, Patrick muttered under his breath:

"Welcome to Maxime Touré's kingdom. Let's hope he's in a generous mood."

The gates shut behind them with the finality of steel teeth. The Prado rolled forward along a shaded driveway lined with flame trees and marble statues that felt out of place in the Guinean heat – classical, European, expensive. They were meant to send a message.

Maxime Touré wasn't just wealthy.

He was curated.

The estate itself rose in tiers – a wide villa of ochre walls and dark wood shutters, flanked by two smaller outbuildings that looked more like military barracks than guest quarters. Private security stood at discrete intervals, holding rifles with the same ease chefs held knives.

Patrick killed the engine.

"Remember," he said softly, "Maxime trusts slowly and hates quickly."

Kadiatu raised an eyebrow. "That's encouraging."

Michael got out of the vehicle and scanned the grounds. No obvious cameras. Which meant the place was wired to hell.

Two guards approached. Tall. Muscular. Silent.

One looked at Patrick. "Monsieur Touré is waiting."

Patrick nodded. "Then let's not make him wait longer."

They were escorted into the villa, where the temperature dropped noticeably – air conditioning so cold it felt deliberate, a reminder that Maxime had power to spare. The interior was a study in contradictions: mahogany furniture beside woven Mano rugs, French abstract paintings hung above West

African ceremonial masks. Beautiful. Chaotic. Expensively curated.

They were brought to a large room overlooking the gardens.

And there he was.

Maxime Touré.

He sat in a high-backed chair as though it were a throne, wearing linen trousers, a loose cream shirt, and flip-flops that somehow looked more expensive than a presidential motorcade. His hair was swept back, his beard immaculate, his eyes sharp enough to slice through lies.

"Patrick," he said, voice smooth as old whisky. "You look exhausted. That usually means you're hiding something."

Patrick gave an almost apologetic shrug. "Only from everyone who isn't you."

Maxime smiled. "Flattery? That's the first warning sign."

His attention slid to Michael.

"So," Maxime said slowly, "this is the ghost."

Michael met the gaze without blinking. "Depends on who you ask."

Maxime laughed softly. "Good. I like men who don't grovel." His voice lowered. "Umbra has been searching for you."

Michael held still. "So I've been told."

"They must consider you valuable." Maxime tapped his fingertips together. "Or dangerous. The distinction is thin."

Kadiatu stepped forward. "We need information."

Maxime glanced at her with mild interest. "And you are?"

"Kadiatu Kamara."

"Ah," he said. "The woman who shot a man through a palm tree in Kailahun two years ago."

Kadiatu stiffened. "That report was sealed."

"Reports bore me," Maxime said. "The truth rarely does."

Aïcha moved past the guards and joined them, her presence shifting the room's balance immediately.

"Maxime," she said.

"Aïcha." He leaned back. "You owe me two favours and one apology."

"You'll get the favours," she replied. "The apology is conditional."

Maxime chuckled. "I'd expect nothing less."

Michael crossed his arms. "You know why we're here."

"Oh, I know why Patrick is here," Maxime said. "He always arrives when his past catches up to him."

His eyes slid back to Michael.

"But you… You're here because the circle has tightened."

"Circle?" Michael asked.

"The ouroboros," Maxime said. "The serpent eating its tail. Umbra's symbol, though they pretend it isn't."

Michael felt the ring in his pocket burn slightly against his palm.

Maxime continued, "Tell me, Michael – how much do you know about the people hunting you?"

Michael stayed silent.

"Exactly," Maxime said. "Not enough."

Aïcha stepped closer to Maxime's chair. "Keita's missing. Umbra took him."

Maxime's expression sobered.

"That," he said, "is unfortunate. Keita was competent. And loyal. Both qualities Umbra enjoys exploiting."

"We want him back," Aïcha said.

Maxime gave a small nod. "Of course you do. And you should. But understand – Umbra never takes without purpose."

"What purpose?" Michael asked.

Maxime drummed a slow rhythm on the arm of his chair.

"Because Keita validated something they didn't want validated. Something he wasn't supposed to see."

Patrick stiffened. "The Black File?"

Maxime looked genuinely amused. "Patrick, Patrick… Still using old names for things that have outgrown them."

"Stop dancing around," Michael said. "Tell us what Umbra is."

Maxime's expression cooled.

"Umbra," he said, "is not a group. Not a cell. Not even an organisation."

He leaned forward.

"Umbra is a sanction."

Michael felt the shift in the room – a pressure, like gravity tightening.

Maxime continued, "Umbra exists only when multiple powerful interests align… briefly… around a shared necessity. Not ideology. Not politics. Necessity."

Kadiatu frowned. "What kind of necessity?"

"The kind that requires speed," Maxime said softly. "Silence. And deniability."

Aïcha's voice lowered. "A kill switch."

Maxime nodded. "Exactly."

Michael leaned forward. "And I'm in their way?"

"You're not in their way," Maxime said. "You are their loose thread. And loose threads unravel tapestries that took years to weave."

Patrick exhaled sharply. "Then we're already compromised."

"No," Maxime said, shaking his head. "You're not compromised."

His eyes found Michael again.

"You're targeted."

Michael didn't flinch. "Then they should hurry."

Maxime barked a laugh. "Oh, they will."

He rose with the languid confidence of a man who feared nothing on earth.

"But before they do… I have something for you."

He nodded to one of the guards.

The guard stepped forward, carrying a small metal case.

He placed it gently on the table.

Maxime gestured to it lightly. "Inside that box is why Keita was taken. Why Umbra is hunting you. Why the Pastor never mattered."

Michael stared at the case.

Patrick's breath caught.

Aïcha's eyes sharpened into blades.

Kadiatu whispered, "What did he find?"

Maxime's voice dropped to a murmur.

"The truth," he said. "And the truth is always dangerous."

Maxime flipped the latches on the metal case with slow, deliberate precision – the kind of ritual a man performs only when unveiling something that changes the room it enters. The lid creaked open.

Inside was a black tablet, inert, wrapped in a static-proof sleeve, and beside it, a small drive encased in hardened titanium.

Maxime tapped the drive. "Keita decrypted half of this before Umbra paid him a visit. The other half is locked behind a sequence buried so deep that even my people can't brute-force it."

Patrick leaned over the table. "What's on it?"

Maxime didn't answer immediately. Instead he turned the tablet on.

The screen flickered. A loading wheel spun. Then a map appeared – stark, white, clinical – with concentric circles radiating out from a point on the West African coast.

Michael frowned. "What am I looking at?"

Maxime zoomed in.

The epicentre was not Sierra Leone.

Not Guinea.

Not Liberia.

It was Bonthe District, south of Sherbro Island – the Pastor's territory.

A new icon appeared on the map. A flashing red marker labelled:

ECLIPSE PROTOCOL – PHASE 1 ASSET ALLOCATION

Michael felt the skin along his forearms tighten.

Maxime said nothing, letting the weight of the words settle.

Kadiatu leaned forward. "Eclipse Protocol? I've never heard of it."

"You wouldn't," Maxime replied. "It isn't military. It isn't intelligence. It isn't corporate." He glanced at Michael. "It's what forms when interests overlap – money, ideology, fear, and power. Umbra is simply the hand that enforces it."

Patrick swallowed. "So what is Phase 1?"

Maxime slid to the next screen.

A list appeared.

Port upgrades – classified vendor

Airfield runway expansion – expedited

Fuel depot purchases – anonymous consortium

Communications black-site nodes – four active

Paramilitary training cycles – foreign instructors

Satellite bandwidth rental – encrypted spectrum

Each line linked back to Umbra's ghost network of shifting companies and false fronts.

And each arrow pointed toward one man.

The Pastor.

Michael exhaled slowly. "This isn't a militia. This is an infrastructure project."

Maxime nodded. "Exactly." His voice dropped. "And infrastructure has purpose."

Aïcha's expression hardened. "Keita must have connected two threads."

"He did," Maxime said. "And Umbra realised he'd seen too much."

He zoomed further.

At the bottom of the screen was a final entry:

PHASE 2 – TARGET ACQUISITION & REMOVAL

Priority: HIGH

Subject: M. / Internal designation: REDHAWK

The room froze.

Michael's mind didn't.

He understood instantly.

Umbra wasn't just reacting to him.

Umbra was building toward him.

Aïcha broke the silence. "They've marked you for removal."

Patrick added, "With clandestine clearance."

Kadiatu spoke last, voice low. "This is a death warrant. Sanitised. Officially invisible."

Maxime pressed the tablet off. "Keita found the link between your extraction from Sierra Leone, the cocoa farm data node, and Umbra's satellite hops. He didn't know what you had done to attract their attention. But he knew you were in the wire."

Michael leaned back, expression unreadable.

"Why me?"

"Because you're the only one who walked away from Cotonou," Maxime answered.

Patrick flinched as though struck.

Michael's jaw clenched. "That was an operation. A disaster. A cluster of bad intel and worse leadership."

"Precisely," Maxime said softly. "And you survived it. Men like you are not supposed to walk away from events designed to burn the ground clean."

Michael's voice lowered. "Designed by whom?"

Maxime met his eyes. "Umbra placed assets in Cotonou. You disrupted them without knowing. They don't forgive disruption."

Kadiatu looked between them. "So this whole thing – Sierra Leone, the Pastor, the mercenaries – it's all tied to Cotonou?"

"No," Maxime said. "Cotonou was the spark. Eclipse Protocol is the fire."

Aïcha spoke next, her voice steady. "There's more, isn't there?"

"Yes," Maxime said, pulling a final paper from the case – crumpled, stained, written in Keita's hurried hand.

It read:

"HE SAW THE ARCHITECTS."

Michael frowned. "Architects?"

Maxime tapped the serpent ring on Michael's palm.

"The ones who built Umbra."

The word architects hung in the air like smoke.

Patrick stepped back. "You mean the consortium?"

Maxime smiled faintly. "I mean something older than that. Something above it. The Consortium is a tool. Umbra is a mechanism. But the architects–"

He didn't finish.

Because someone outside screamed.

Not a cry of pain.

A warning.

Gunfire shredded the air a split second later – sharp, precise, controlled bursts.

Patrick ducked. "We're compromised!"

Kadiatu drew her pistol. "How the hell did Umbra find us?"

Aïcha's jaw tightened. "Because Maxime's house is a lighthouse. Everyone sees who goes in."

Maxime didn't argue. He snapped the case shut. "Move. We go out the east corridor."

Another burst tore through the windows, glass exploding inward.

Michael grabbed the ring, shoved the drive into his pocket, and pulled Kadiatu toward cover.

A shadow moved past the window – fluid, fast, silent.

Not militia.

Not local muscle.

Umbra kill-team.

Maxime's estate, for all its walls and guards, was a gilded box.

And Umbra had just prised the lid open.

"Michael!" Patrick shouted. "We need you at the back!"

Michael spun toward the hallway.

A figure was silhouetted against the doorway – tall, still, wearing combat blacks.

And on his finger, glinting in the fractured light…

A serpent ring.

Michael didn't hesitate.

He fired first.

The figure dropped.

More shadows surged behind him.

Maxime barked, "Move!"

The villa erupted into chaos.

Umbra had come to finish Phase 2.

For a moment, the only sound was the ringing in Michael's ears – a high, metallic hum left behind by close gunfire. Then the world snapped sharply back into motion.

Patrick grabbed Michael's arm. "Move! We have thirty seconds before they breach again."

Maxime was already halfway down the east corridor, pulling a concealed panel on the wall. "This way!"

Kadiatu supported Aïcha – who was limping slightly but refusing help – while Jonas, pale and unsteady, staggered behind them after forcing himself out of the safehouse vehicle. He'd insisted on coming inside when the shots began. Stubborn bastard.

The concealed panel swung open, revealing a narrow service passage lined with power cables and concrete dust.

Michael hustled everyone inside. "Go!"

The moment they entered, Maxime slammed the panel shut.

Darkness swallowed them.

Patrick flicked on a small tactical torch. The beam cut a narrow path ahead.

"Where does this lead?" Kadiatu whispered.

"A utility corridor," Maxime said. "It runs beneath the estate. Built during the French years. No one outside my inner circle knows it exists."

Michael glanced back. "Umbra has a habit of knowing everything."

Maxime didn't disagree. "Then let us hope they're late to the party, just this once."

Behind them, the heavy thud of boots reverberated through the villa floor. Glass shattered. Shouts echoed – crisp, foreign, keyed to encrypted comms.

Michael caught fragments through the floorboards:

"Zulu-One in position."

"No movement south wing."

"Confirm objective location."

"Engage on mark."

Patrick stiffened. "That's Tier-One phrasing."

Maxime looked grim. "Umbra does not send amateurs."

The tunnel dipped, following the slant of the terrain toward the lower gardens. Thick roots broke through the concrete here and there like skeletal fingers. The air smelled of damp earth and an old electricity leak.

A sudden metallic crack echoed behind them.

Michael turned sharply.

"Kadiatu – torch!"

She swung her light back.

A hairline fracture was spidering across the concrete wall – from impact.

Umbra had found the hidden passage.

"Faster," Michael growled.

They sprinted.

Jonas stumbled, but Aïcha hooked his arm over her shoulder and dragged him without breaking stride. Patrick ran close to Michael, breathing hard but steady.

Maxime led with unsettling calm, as though accustomed to navigating his estate under fire.

The tunnel split at a Y-section.

Maxime pointed right. "This one."

"Why not the left?" Kadiatu asked.

"Because the left leads to the armoury," Maxime said. "Which they assumed I'd run to. And which they are very likely already flooding with men."

Another explosion tore through the passage behind them, showering them with dust.

The lights flickered – then died completely.

"Run!" Michael shouted.

They plunged into darkness, feet pounding, walls brushing their shoulders in the black.

Then – faint light.

Daylight.

The passage opened to a maintenance hatch set into a hillside below the estate. Maxime threw it open and spilled out onto a slope covered in wild grass and tangled vines.

Fresh air hit them like a slap.

"Keep low," Patrick hissed.

As they cleared the hatch, Michael heard the first sweep of rotor blades overhead – low, fast, deliberate.

A helicopter.

He grabbed Maxime's shirt. "Did you call in anything?"

Maxime shook his head. "No."

"Then that's not ours."

The helicopter banked, its silhouette cutting across the sky – matte black, narrow profile, military-grade. A spotlight burst on, slicing through the trees.

Michael shoved everyone into the brush. "Down!"

The beam swept once. Twice. Then settled over the estate.

Kadiatu whispered, "They're searching for bodies."

"No," Michael said. "They're confirming kills."

The beam lingered.

Then the helicopter veered north and disappeared beyond the ridge.

"Move," Michael said through clenched teeth. "We have minutes, not hours."

Maxime guided them into the trees, following a narrow path concealed beneath brush and fallen palm fronds.

"This leads to the lower road," he said. "I keep a secondary vehicle there."

Patrick muttered, "Thank God for your paranoia."

"Paranoia keeps me alive," Maxime replied. "Arrogance kills men like Umbra."

They wound deeper into the forest, the sound of insects rising around them like static. Branches snapped underfoot. Sweat stung their eyes. The air was thick and moist – a jungle in miniature.

A rustle cut through the noise.

Michael raised a hand. "Stop."

Everyone froze.

Silence.

Then – a whisper of movement.

A figure stepped from behind a tree.

Not Umbra.

A boy. No older than fourteen. Thin, barefoot, holding a bag of charcoal slung over his shoulder.

He stared at them, wide-eyed.

Michael lowered his weapon. "Hey–"

Before he could finish, Maxime stepped forward, knelt, and pressed a folded note into the boy's hand.

"Run home," Maxime said softly. "Now."

The boy nodded once, terrified, then vanished into the brush.

Kadiatu exhaled. "You scared him half to death."

"No," Maxime said. "I paid him to forget."

The path opened suddenly onto a narrow dirt road. A weathered Land Cruiser sat tucked beneath a cluster of banana leaves.

Maxime unlocked it with a click.

"Everyone in," he commanded.

They piled inside – Michael in the passenger seat this time, Patrick and Aïcha in the middle row, Kadiatu and Jonas in the back.

Maxime started the engine.

But before he put the car in gear, he spoke without looking at any of them.

"You must listen to me."

The tone was wrong. Too flat. Too direct.

Michael tensed. "What is it?"

Maxime looked straight ahead, knuckles whitening on the steering wheel.

"Umbra is not hunting you because of what you know," he said softly. "They're hunting you because of what you were supposed to become."

Michael's pulse tightened. "Meaning?"

Maxime turned to him.

"You were meant to be an asset," he said. "One they could shape. One they could use. Cotonou wasn't your failure. It was your test. And you passed in the wrong direction."

Silence fell like a blade.

"What direction is that?" Michael asked.

Maxime's gaze hardened.

"The one where you stayed human."

Behind them, faint in the distance, the helicopter turned back.

And this time, it was coming straight toward them.

"Seatbelts," Michael said. "Now."

Maxime slammed the accelerator.

The trees exploded into motion as the Land Cruiser tore down the dirt road, dust rising in a long plume behind them.

Umbra had found them again.

And Chapter Six would begin with the chase.

Chapter 6

THE ROAD THROUGH SAMU

"A snake that forgets its old skin is easy to catch."
– African proverb

The hills north of Conakry were still dark when Michael left the safehouse, the diesel generator coughing behind him like an old smoker. The air tasted of dust and salt – the last breath of the Atlantic carried inland before morning heat flattened it. He adjusted the strap of his pack, settled his weight, and started toward the waiting motorcycle.

It wasn't a good bike. It wasn't even a reliable bike.

But it was the kind of machine that slipped through borderlands without being noticed, the sort used by farmers, smugglers and men with nowhere official to be.

Patrick had laid out the plan the night before, tension pulling at the edges of his voice.

"Stay off the main road. Avoid checkpoints. Don't make contact unless you have to."

Michael had nodded, though they both knew that nothing involving Samu – or Umbra – was ever that simple.

Now, as he kicked the engine to life and felt the machine shudder beneath him, he understood the real reason Patrick hadn't come along. The man feared what they might find in those old training grounds. And Michael… Michael feared what he might remember.

He eased onto the road while the horizon shifted from charcoal to pale blue. Conakry fell away behind him – its bustle, its noise, its sea-salt chaos – until only the long rural road remained. The landscape opened into low scrubland, broken by clusters of mango trees and the occasional mud-brick village. Women swept courtyards. Men carried bundles under their arms. Goats drifted lazily across the track as if daring vehicles to try their luck.

After an hour, the sun began to assert itself–warm at first, then aggressive. Michael loosened the collar of his shirt and let the wind carry the sweat from his neck. The monotony of the road gave him space to think, though he wasn't sure that was an advantage.

He saw flashes of the night before:

Maxime's estate under attack.

The helicopter banking through smoke.

Jonas and Aïcha forcing themselves to run despite pain and blood and exhaustion.

Umbra had moved with precision.

Too precise.

This was no hunt. It was an extraction attempt gone wrong.

If they had wanted all of them dead, the estate would have been flattened. Instead, they'd sent in a surgical team, timed to hit while Keita's data was being revealed. Umbra wanted the team splintered, not erased.

Divide.

Scatter.

Isolate.

Now here he was, riding toward a place with a history of death and secrets, carrying nothing but a coin he didn't understand and a message that made no sense.

Testify.

He replayed the word again.

A warning?

A command?

A threat?

Or the start of a story Michael didn't yet have the beginning of?

As the sun climbed higher, the road narrowed into a rough dirt path flanked by tall, dry grass. The motorcycle growled unhappily at every rut. Insects flitted across the track, their wings catching the light like sparks. The heat pressed down on him, thick, relentless.

An hour later, he stopped at a roadside stall – little more than a tarp stretched over wooden poles. A young man with tired eyes watched him approach. Michael bought a sachet of water, tearing it open with his teeth as he leaned against the bike.

"You go Kambia side?" the man asked.

"Something like that."

The man nodded slowly. "Careful today. Soldiers moving."

"Where?"

He shrugged. "Everywhere."

Michael finished the water and mounted the bike again.

Soldiers, or men pretending to be soldiers – in this region, the distinction was blurred.

The road wound into a stretch of forest. Palm fronds arched overhead, filtering the sunlight into broken shards that danced over the path. The soundscape changed – insects buzzing lower, birds calling warily from the canopy. The forest felt alive, but watchful.

Then the old training trails began.

The ground bore scars from years of drills, tyres, boots and worse. Michael slowed, letting instinct take the lead. These were the roads where the pre-war and post-war generations of Sierra Leonean security forces had been hardened – or broken. Samu was a place where reformers tried to teach restraint, and warlords tried to teach obedience.

And some men learnt both.

A cluster of burned-out vehicles appeared on the left – relics from a riot-control exercise long abandoned. Bullet holes peppered the metal. Rust had eaten the doors. Children once played in these shells. Now no one came this far without reason.

The path narrowed until the branches brushed his arms. The bike snarled as he coaxed it forward over exposed roots. Sweat stung his eyes. The hum of insects grew louder.

Then the forest dipped and opened into a clearing.

Samu.

The old public order training base sat hunched like a wounded animal – concrete walls cracked, roofs sagging, paint peeled away by sun and rain. Watchtowers leaned just slightly off true, like men trying not to show weakness.

The place had always been haunted, but today the silence was heavier. Not peaceful. Not empty.

Held.

Michael killed the engine and listened.

No birdsong.

No voices.

No movement of air.

The base wasn't abandoned.

It was occupied – carefully, quietly, and with intent.

He dismounted and rolled the bike behind a cluster of brush. The earth was dry and sun-baked, but recent tracks marked the clearing – tyre impressions, boot prints, two sets of footprints that didn't match local shoes. The print pattern was wrong – foreign tactical soles, light but deep.

Someone had arrived before him.

Someone disciplined.

Michael moved toward the edge of the compound, keeping to the shadows. A faint scent lingered in the air – cordite, sweat, and something metallic. Not blood. Machinery, perhaps. Or oil.

He crouched behind an old concrete barrier, listening again.

Still nothing.

Too still.

Then – a crack, soft and heavy, like a footstep on old wood.

Michael froze.

Another sound followed – deliberate, slow, confident.

Not the idle pacing of local youths or smugglers.

A watcher.

He lowered himself even further, eyes scanning the towers. The sun glared off the rusted railings. Shadows cut across the interior yard in jagged shapes.

A shape moved between them.

Not enough to identify.

Just enough to confirm he was no longer alone.

Michael steadied his breathing.

Samu was awake.

And it was watching him back.

Michael remained perfectly still, one hand resting lightly on the ground, feeling for vibration as much as listening for sound. The watcher inside the compound moved with the casual certainty of someone who knew the terrain intimately. A veteran, then – or someone trained to become one.

He shifted his weight and slipped along the tree line, keeping the broken wall in sight. The morning sun had begun to harden, burning away the last remnants of dawn's coolness. Sweat gathered at the base of his neck.

Another movement, this time a shadow breaking rhythm across the far barracks block.

One watcher.

Possibly two.

No voices.

No idle chatter.

This wasn't a squad. It was a pair of sentries deliberately placed.

A sign of discipline – and purpose.

Michael's fingers brushed against the coin in his pocket, the one left mysteriously in his room back in Coyah. His instincts tightened around the memory of it: the weight of the metal, the inscription, the message it implied.

Testify.

He hadn't made sense of it yet – but Samu was not a place where coincidences occurred without orchestration.

He circled toward the northern fence, where the jungle encroached more aggressively. Creepers had begun reclaiming sections of the wire mesh. A fallen branch created an opening just wide enough for a man to slip through with care.

He studied the gap.

Recent scuff marks.

Not many.

But enough.

Someone else had come this way – someone light-footed and aware of being followed.

Michael sank lower and eased himself forward.

Before he reached the fence, he heard a soft, controlled exhale.

A human sound. Close.

He pivoted silently behind a tree, muscles coiled.

Then – another breath. This one tighter. Measured. A sound made by someone forcing themselves to remain calm.

Michael scanned the undergrowth, eyes adjusting to the fractured light.

There – ten metres ahead, half-hidden behind the trunk of an old palm, a figure knelt with a rifle raised, body angled toward the same gap in the fence.

A local?

Unlikely.

The posture was too precise.

He studied the silhouette: narrow shoulders, compact frame, braided hair tucked beneath a headscarf. Clothing mismatched – civilian trousers but tactical knee pads, old trainers but a high-grade sling on the rifle.

This was no militia kid.

As if sensing his gaze, the figure shifted slightly.

Michael remained still.

Then the rifle lowered, just a fraction.

"Michael Sillah," a woman's voice murmured, low but steady.

He felt the air leave his lungs – not from shock, but from confirmation. Whoever she was, she knew his name, his presence, and the moment he would arrive.

She turned her head enough for him to see her face: narrow, sharp features, dark eyes, skin marked with old dust and new sweat.

"You're late," she whispered.

Michael didn't move. "Who are you?"

"Someone who watched the watchers," she replied.

She nodded toward the compound. "Two inside. Neither very patient."

Michael stepped slightly from cover but kept his hands visible.

"Name," he said quietly.

She hesitated – not out of fear, but calculation.

"Fatmata," she said finally. "Or Fatu. Depends who's asking."

"And you're here because…?"

She exhaled softly. "Because Samu isn't empty. And because someone wanted you to see that."

Michael studied her more carefully. She was trained – not in a formal military sense, but in survival, reconnaissance, and the sort of intelligence-gathering that came from growing up in unstable regions where knowing too much could kill you and knowing too little could kill you faster.

"Who sent you?" he asked.

"No one," she said. "I came because I'm tired of pretending this place is just an old ruin."

Her eyes cut toward the compound again. "They came three days ago. Brought supplies. Weapons. No insignia. No local dialect."

Foreigners.

Exactly what he'd feared.

Michael crouched beside her. "How many total?"

"Four, maybe five," she whispered. "But only two stay visible. The others move after dark."

He nodded. "What have they been doing?"

"Listening," she said. "Waiting."

"For what?"

Her gaze slid to him. "For you."

A chill rippled down his spine despite the heat.

He kept his voice steady. "You're sure?"

"I saw one of them holding a photo," she said. "Not clear, but… close enough."

Michael didn't allow the hit to show on his face.

"Why warn me?" he asked.

"Because I know what happens when strangers build shadows in our country," she said. "They don't leave until the ground is stained."

He absorbed that quietly.

Fatmata steadied her rifle and nodded toward the fence. "You want to get inside, you go now. They'll change positions soon."

Michael considered it. Going inside meant confronting whatever was waiting – or whoever was watching from deeper darkness.

Fatmata seemed to read his hesitation.

"I'll cover you," she added.

"You don't even know me."

"I know the kind of man Umbra hunts," she replied. "And if they want you dead, you're probably the only one around here worth saving."

It wasn't comfort.

It was simply the truth.

Michael exhaled once, deeply, and slipped through the gap in the fence.

As the jungle swallowed him and Fatmata's figure blurred into green and shadow behind him, he felt the full weight of Samu's silence settle around his shoulders.

He was no longer approaching the past.

He had stepped directly into its jaws.

The air inside the compound felt heavier, as if the heat itself had conspired with the concrete to trap every sound, every memory, every ghost that had ever walked these training grounds. Michael moved slowly, his boots barely disturbing the dust as he crossed into the shadow of the collapsed watchtower.

Samu hadn't changed as much as it had decayed.

But it hadn't died.

The silence wasn't absence.

It was pressure.

The kind that built before storms – or ambushes.

He kept low, scanning the angles, checking the corners that once formed the backbone of riot and public order drills. The wide central yard lay open under the hardening sun, its cracked surface scattered with debris: a broken baton, a rusted shield, a faded training helmet half-swallowed by dirt.

He moved toward one of the long blocks that used to house supply rooms. A door hung half-open at the far end, creaking gently. Not enough wind for that, he noted. Someone had moved through recently.

He reached the doorway and paused.

Listened.

Nothing.

He eased the door wider with the tip of his fingers.

Inside, sunlight bled through gaps in the corrugated roof, striping the room with pale gold. Old lockers lined the left wall. Dust lay thick across the floor. But near the centre, something disrupted the uniform layer – a set of boot prints, heavier than Fatmata's, deep and deliberate.

He crouched, touched the rim of one. Still fresh.

Then he saw it – a small mark carved into the concrete just beside the print. A circle with a diagonal line through it.

Military marking.

Foreign.

Non-NATO.

He'd seen similar etchings once during joint operations in Namibia – symbols used by private military groups to identify cleared sectors.

Umbra-adjacent groups.

Or their imitators.

He stood slowly. The stillness pressed closer.

A soft metallic scrape sliced through the silence.

Michael drew back behind the doorframe as a figure entered the room from the opposite side.

Broad shoulders.

Rifle raised.

Movements clean, silent, methodical.

Umbra.

The man paused near the lockers, scanning the room. His posture radiated a cold patience – the kind possessed by operators trained to eliminate targets quietly, efficiently.

Michael remained perfectly still, heart steady, breaths measured.

The man moved further inside.

Three steps.

Four.

Michael waited until the angle shifted – until the shadow of the rifle barrel tracked just a fraction too far left.

Then he moved.

Silent.

Swift.

He closed the distance and drove his forearm against the man's wrist, knocking the rifle off line. The operator reacted fast – spinning, elbow rising – but Michael deflected the strike and rammed his shoulder into the man's centre mass, forcing him back.

They crashed against a locker, metal clanging like a weak alarm.

The operator swung a knife up from his belt – fast, close, lethal.

Michael twisted, the blade skimming past his ribs. He seized the man's wrist, pivoted sharply, and slammed his elbow down. Bone cracked.

The man grunted but didn't drop the knife.

Highly trained.

Very highly trained.

Michael drove his knee into the man's thigh, disrupting his balance. Another wrench of the arm and the knife fell, clattering to the concrete.

The operator reached for his sidearm.

Michael was faster.

He grabbed the back of the man's head and smashed it into the locker. Once. Twice.

The body sagged.

Michael held him against the metal until the limbs stopped resisting.

He lowered the man quietly and checked the insignia on the inside of the collar.

Unmarked.

Of course.

But the ring on the left hand–

He froze.

A serpent devouring its tail.

Umbra.

He stared at it longer than he meant to – not out of fear, but recognition. This was the same ring design he'd been forced to wear briefly years ago, during Cotonou, during the operation they had sabotaged, reshaped, and buried beneath layers of redactions.

He pulled the ring free and pocketed it.

Another footstep echoed outside.

Michael shifted back into the shadows.

A second operator?

Fatmata hadn't mentioned any on perimeter.

Which meant this one had looped around from the south block.

He readied himself.

But the footstep didn't come closer. Instead, it stopped abruptly. A soft exhale followed – then stillness.

Michael angled himself toward the doorway.

A body lay half-slumped beside the wall outside. A clean, precise gunshot wound through the forehead.

And beside it, footprints leading away – smaller, lighter, faster.

Fatmata.

She had taken the second man.

Michael stepped over the body and followed the prints. They led toward the old parade ground, then angled sharply toward the far training pit.

He passed an old sign half-buried in dust:

OSD TRAINING ZONE – AUTHORITY ONLY

He remembered standing under that sign years ago, delivering briefings to officers who were too young, too tired, or too broken to care about chain of command. He wondered how many of them had survived long enough to regret those days.

As he approached the training pit, he saw her – Fatmata – crouched near a low wall, her rifle trained on the barracks beyond.

She didn't look back. "Two more inside the east block," she whispered.

Michael crouched beside her. "You're sure?"

"They were arguing," she said. "One wanted to pull out. The other wanted to wait."

"Wait for what?"

Her voice tightened. "For confirmation."

The word struck him harder than he expected.

Confirmation of what?

His arrival?

His death?

Or the completion of some mission Umbra hadn't yet revealed?

He steadied his thoughts. "We take them quietly."

Fatmata nodded. "I'll take left."

"No," Michael said. "You cover. I go in."

She shot him a sharp look. "You don't know the layout."

"I used to train officers here."

Her expression changed – shock, then something close to respect.

"Then go," she said, settling deeper into her firing position. "I'll keep you breathing."

Michael moved toward the east block, stepping through long shadows cast by the rising sun. The air grew thicker, as if the compound itself held its breath.

Inside Samu, danger had always been a teacher.

Today, it had returned to give a lesson of its own.

Michael entered the east block through a doorway half-swallowed by creeping vines. The interior was dim, lit only by thin shafts of sunlight slicing through holes in the roof. Dust floated in slow spirals, disturbed only when he passed through them.

This building had once housed riot gear, tear-gas canisters, and protective equipment. Now it smelled of sweat, old canvas, and the faint chemical tang of weapons cleaning oil.

Voices murmured deeper inside.

Low. Controlled. Not local dialect.

Michael hugged the wall and moved toward the sound, pausing near a collapsed storage rack.

"...confirmation still pending," one voice said – crisp, irritated.

Another responded, calmer. "HQ is prioritising redundancy. You saw what happened at Coyah."

A pause.

"Two teams lost. They want certainty before extraction."

Extraction.

Not elimination.

Michael shifted closer.

The calmer voice continued, "Our orders are simple. Hold position. Secure the ground. Wait for Redhawk's trajectory."

Michael's jaw tightened.

Redhawk.

His designation again.

He moved one step further – just enough to see the two operators through the fractured doorway into the next room.

The first stood near a dusty table, rifle slung loose, pacing with impatience.

The second sat on an overturned crate, assembling a small metallic device that looked too clean, too modern, for a place like Samu.

Michael recognised the shape immediately.

A signal repeater.

Military-grade.

Short-range.

Encrypted.

Used for triangulating targets in dense terrain.

They weren't just tracking him.

They were mapping him.

He drew a slow breath.

One step.

Two.

A plank creaked underfoot.

The pacing operator turned sharply. "You hear that–?"

Michael moved.

He crossed the room in three strides and slammed the first man into the wall before the rifle could swing up. The second leapt to his feet, grabbing for a sidearm.

Michael drove his elbow into the first operator's throat, then ducked as the second fired – the shot punching a splintered hole through the wooden frame behind him.

He knocked over the table, sending the signal repeater skittering across the floor.

The second operator lunged.

Michael met him halfway.

They grappled, the man stronger than expected, trained and efficient. His forearm locked around Michael's neck, squeezing with brutal precision.

Michael twisted, drove his heel into the man's knee, then slammed the back of his head into the operator's face. Bone cracked. The grip loosened.

He wrenched free and struck once, twice – fast, decisive – until the man collapsed to his knees and stayed there.

The first operator, stunned but conscious, reached for something on his vest.

Michael pinned his wrist and pressed him against the wall.

"What is Umbra doing here?" Michael growled.

The man spat blood. "Too late."

"For what?"

The operator smiled through cracked teeth. "The next phase."

"What phase?"

His smile widened – wrong, eerie, certain.

"The one you can't stop."

Michael drove a sharp blow into his jaw, dropping him unconscious. He turned toward the fallen repeater and crouched beside it.

The device was still active – a small blinking indicator pulsing green.

He picked it up carefully.

A faint hum vibrated through the casing.

Not a tracker.

A beacon.

A locator for something much larger.

A rustle came from the doorway behind him.

He spun.

Fatmata.

Her rifle was raised, but her eyes were on the repeater.

"What is that?" she asked.

"Not good," Michael said. "Umbra wasn't waiting for me. They were anchoring something. Setting a marker."

"For what?"

He slid the repeater into his bag. "I don't know. Not yet."

Fatmata glanced at the unconscious men. "More will come."

"I know."

She moved to the window slit and scanned the tree line. "You hear that?"

Michael listened.

For a moment, nothing.

Then –

Distant engines.

Not vehicles.

Not bikes.

Aircraft.

Low.

Fast.

Approaching from the west.

Michael's chest went cold.

"They're bringing something in," Fatmata whispered. "Something heavy."

Michael stepped back into the corridor, checking sight lines. "We need to move. Now."

They exited the east block and crossed the yard, staying wide of the tower. Fatmata kept her rifle trained high; Michael covered the rear.

At the edge of the compound, he retrieved the motorcycle from the brush.

Fatmata frowned. "They'll hear you coming."

"They already know I'm here."

She hesitated, then slung her rifle. "Then I'm coming too."

"No," Michael said. "This road gets worse before it gets better."

"Good," she replied, climbing onto the back of the bike. "I'm worse too."

He didn't argue.

He kicked the engine alive.

As the motorcycle jolted forward, the aircraft roar grew louder overhead.

Fatmata gripped his shoulder. "They're circling. They're looking for something."

Michael gunned the throttle as they burst through the clearing and shot down the dirt track.

"They're not looking," he said.

"They're confirming."

"Confirming what?"

"That Phase Two has begun."

The track narrowed into choking brush. Branches tore at their clothes. Dust billowed behind them.

Then, as they broke free onto the long straight stretch leading back toward the road, something caught Michael's eye in the rear-view mirror.

A flare of reflected light.

Then another.

Vehicles.

Two.

Maybe three.

Closing fast.

Fatmata leaned close. "You said we needed to move."

"We are."

"Then move faster."

Michael nodded and twisted the throttle until the engine shrieked beneath them.

The bike shot forward into the heat, the wilderness blurring into streaks of green and red laterite.

Behind them, Umbra gave chase.

And the old Samu base – long abandoned by officials, long forgotten by reformers – had awakened once more, its ghosts now stretching out into the world beyond.

CHAPTER 7

THE WEIGHT OF WITNESSES

"When a tree falls in the forest, the birds don't mourn; they relocate."
– AFRICAN PROVERB

The road out of Samu burned under the morning sun, the heat rising in warped, shimmering sheets that made the distance look fluid and uncertain. Michael rode until the compound and its watchers disappeared behind the curtain of dust. Fatmata's grip on his shoulder didn't loosen until they reached the wider track, where the forest began to thin and the horizon opened into pale, smoke-washed sky.

He slowed the motorcycle enough for her to release her breath – a long, shaky exhale she'd been holding for too long.

"You didn't have to come with me," he said.

"I know." Her voice was steady now, the adrenaline fading into something sharper. "But they weren't there by accident. And Samu isn't just a memory anymore. It's becoming something."

He nodded. "Something organised."

"Something coming," she corrected.

The track widened into a rough junction where a cluster of roadside vendors sold gari, dried fish, and plastic jerrycans of fuel. The kind of place where news passed in whispers and danger travelled faster than vehicles. Michael pulled over, killing the engine.

Fatmata swung off the bike and adjusted her headscarf. "You should rest. Drink water."

"I'm fine."

"You look like a man who forgot what resting feels like."

He didn't argue.

He bought a sachet of water from an old woman who watched him with eyes that had seen far too many shifting tides of authority. The moment he lowered the sachet, she murmured:

"You came from the old camp."

It wasn't a question.

Michael froze. "Not much left there."

"There's always something left. Especially in places where men shouted and spirits listened."

Fatmata shot him a look that said: I told you this place carries ghosts.

Michael returned to the bike. "I need to move."

"Where?" she asked.

"Kambia first. Then Freetown, if I can make it."

Fatmata frowned. "If they were waiting for you at Samu, they'll watch the borders."

"I know."

"You'll need help."

Michael tightened his grip on the handlebars. "I'm used to being outnumbered."

"That's not help. That's memory."

He allowed himself a small, tired breath. "Fatmata–"

She stepped back, cutting him off gently. "You go. I'll disappear for a while. They don't know me. Not yet."

He reached for the ignition.

She reached for his wrist.

"Michael," she said quietly, "whatever they're doing at Samu… it's not just for you."

Her tone carried weight – the kind that came from people who'd lived through wars others only read about. The kind that didn't embellish.

The kind that warned.

He nodded once, then rode.

Two hours later, the road north bent toward the mangrove belt. The smell of brine returned, thicker now, as if the Atlantic itself were following him inland. He crossed a wooden bridge that creaked under the weight of the motorcycle and pushed on until the scrubland shifted back into forest.

The heat became oppressive – not just physical, but atmospheric, like the air had thickened enough to slow thought.

Gibril emerged from the back of Michael's mind with unwelcome clarity.

Not as the man who once stood beside him during the coup attempt.

Not as the reckless, brilliant officer with a gift for tactics and a taste for edges.

But as the rumour –

The ghost who had resurfaced in transit hubs across Europe.

Berlin.

Istanbul.

Trieste.

A man who should have been in hiding, yet moved with the confidence of someone carrying protection – or purpose.

He hadn't vanished, Michael realised.

He had been repositioned.

That thought settled uneasily beneath his ribs.

He rounded a bend, slowing as he neared a checkpoint hastily assembled from oil drums and wooden planks. Two local officers lounged under a tarp, barely paying attention. The motorcycle drew their eyes briefly, but a small bribe and a forged explanation got him through with minimal scrutiny.

Beyond the checkpoint, the forest opened into a clearing where the dust had been flattened by repeated tyre tracks. Something – or someone – had been operating here recently.

He kept riding.

Eventually, the land dipped toward a small cluster of houses – a quiet, dusty settlement where children played with improvised footballs and men patched fishing nets in the shade of salt-burnt trees.

This was where Vaughan had said they would meet.

Or rather, where Vaughan had implied he could be found.

Michael cut the engine and waited.

The settlement watched him – not with alarm, but with the resigned curiosity given to travellers who looked like they were carrying trouble in invisible bags.

A man emerged from a narrow alley between two houses.

Tall.

Leaning on a cane he didn't need.

Dressed in desert boots and a shirt that didn't belong to this climate.

Vaughan.

Michael didn't stand, but his posture shifted.

Vaughan approached with the kind of unhurried confidence only carried by men who believed nothing could surprise them anymore.

"You look like hell," Vaughan said.

"You look like you're enjoying this," Michael replied.

Vaughan smiled. "I enjoy very little these days. But watching you outrun the consequences of an organisation no one admits exists… that's entertainment."

Michael folded his arms. "You working for them?"

"I've worked for everyone," Vaughan said. "Governments. Contractors. Corporations. People who pretend they're none of the above. The real question is who I'm working for today."

"And today?"

Vaughan's eyes glinted. "Someone who thinks you're not ready to die."

Michael didn't move. "What do you want?"

Vaughan stepped closer, lowering his voice. "To warn you that Samu wasn't an accident. It's a staging ground. A calibration point. They're building something."

Michael's jaw tightened. "For what?"

"For whoever survives the next phase."

"And what's the next phase?"

Vaughan's smile faded.

For the first time, his eyes looked old – not in years, but in burden.

"Redhawk," he said softly. "They don't want to kill you. Not yet."

Michael's pulse hardened. "Then why shadow me?"

"Because some men are too valuable dead," Vaughan murmured. "And far more dangerous alive."

He stepped back.

"And because someone wants you to witness what comes next."

Michael didn't respond immediately. He let Vaughan's words settle, testing them for weight, shape, and motive. The man was too experienced to waste breath on melodrama, and too self-interested to lie without purpose.

"Witness what, exactly?" Michael asked.

Vaughan tilted his head. "You already know the answer."

"I want to hear you say it."

A pause. A long one. The kind that formed when truth felt like a debt.

"Eclipse Protocol," Vaughan said quietly. "You kicked the door open in Samu. You weren't meant to."

Michael frowned. "You think I planned that?"

"I think you're a man who attracts hidden plans like iron attracts magnets."

Vaughan's gaze flicked toward the northern road. "They're aligning things. Samu's one piece. Kambia's another. There are more."

"More sites?"

"More teeth," Vaughan murmured. "Eclipse isn't a single project. It's a pipeline. Sabotage, surveillance, acquisition, displacement… and somewhere down the line, someone gets to decide who becomes useful, and who becomes disposable."

Michael kept his voice level. "You're talking like Umbra is an institution."

"Umbra is whatever the architects need it to be," Vaughan replied. "A sanction. A shadow. A set of hands that appear when the world needs things no one will admit to approving."

Michael studied the settlement around them – women washing clothes in iron basins, children kicking a deflated ball, old men repairing nets with quiet resignation. A normal scene cast under an abnormal shadow.

"And where do you fit in?" he asked.

Vaughan chuckled once, without humour. "I don't fit anywhere. That's why they occasionally hire me."

"Who?"

"Everyone," Vaughan said again. "Umbra. The Consortium. Certain ministries in London that don't like to see their fingerprints on anything. I'm a blunt tool with a flexible handle." He leaned in slightly. "But even I don't like what Samu suggests."

Michael let that sit.

Vaughan tapped his cane lightly against the ground. "Your friend Hassan was looking for you."

Michael stiffened. "Hassan?"

"He's close. He's scared. And he's not wrong." Vaughan's eyes sharpened. "Things are heating up in Freetown. The Americans are twitching, the French are meddling, and certain people in your old command are acting like they already know the ending of a story you haven't even read the first chapter of."

Michael felt a sharp, familiar ache beneath the ribs – the ache of realising that the past he'd outrun hadn't slowed, merely widened its net.

Vaughan straightened. "Hassan's not far. You'll want to hear what he knows."

"What does he know?"

"Enough to die for," Vaughan said simply. "Let's hope he manages to tell you first."

The journey north shifted again, the landscape flattening into open country where the horizon stretched in clean, unbroken lines. Michael rode hard, the motorcycle rattling against rough ground until the track fed gently into a smoother road.

Fatmata's warning lingered behind his thoughts.

Vaughan's words pressed ahead of them.

He followed the route toward a small fuel station on the outskirts of a larger settlement. A tin roof clung to the top of a concrete block structure. A man in a football vest poured petrol into glass jars and sold them like cold drinks.

Hassan was waiting.

He leaned quietly against the wall, his face tired, eyes red-rimmed but alert. He straightened when he saw Michael.

"You look older," Hassan said.

"You look like you've been running," Michael replied.

"I have."

Michael parked the bike and strode toward him. Hassan wasn't usually shaken – not visibly. Today, he looked like a man who'd seen too many shadows moving at once.

"I thought you left the country," Michael said.

"I tried."

"And?"

"Borders feel different," Hassan murmured. "Too many people asking the wrong questions. Some asking about you."

Michael swallowed a sharp breath. "What have you heard?"

"That Samu isn't the only place being used." Hassan glanced around before leaning closer. "They're setting up logistics like it's a campaign. Coordinated. Funded."

"Umbra?"

"Umbra and something else," Hassan whispered. "I saw trucks coming from the coast. No markings. No paperwork. And the men supervising weren't local."

Michael felt the shift the subtle awareness that the ground beneath his feet was beginning to tilt.

"What were they carrying?" he asked.

Hassan hesitated. "People."

A cold line traced down Michael's spine. "Hostages?"

"No." Hassan swallowed. "Recruits. Some willing. Some not."

"Press-ganged?"

"Or bought."

Michael turned away for a moment, pushing down the rising anger. The Atlantic had a long history of taking people from these shores. The idea that a modern shadow network was repeating that cycle filled him with a quiet, lethal heat.

"Hassan," he said finally, "where are they moving them?"

Hassan pointed east. "Toward Port Loko. There's a new checkpoint. Military, but… not military. They had paperwork that looked official but didn't match any unit I recognised."

Michael absorbed that slowly.

"And why look for me?"

Hassan's voice dropped to a whisper.

"Because of Cotonou."

The name struck like a hammer – not in volume, but in weight.

Michael's jaw tightened. "That's done. Buried."

"No," Hassan said. "Someone dug it up."

The world felt momentarily smaller.

Hassan looked around again, anxiety climbing into his voice. "We can't talk here."

Michael nodded. "Then let's go."

Hassan stepped toward the Land Cruiser parked beside the station.

And for a brief moment – a single breath, a thin crack in time – Michael believed they might actually leave this place.

Then a man rose from the back seat.

No insignia.

No expression.

Eyes cold as quiet water.

The muzzle flash was a pulse of white.

Hassan staggered.

Michael reached him before he hit the ground.

Blood seeped quickly across Hassan's shirt – too fast, too dark.

His friend's breath rattled once, catching on the edge of a word that never formed.

"Hassan–"

But the light left his eyes.

Hassan's body slumped heavily against Michael's chest, the weight sudden and final. The world around him muted – sound drained into a dull, submerged hum, as if someone had placed thick glass between him and everything else.

For a moment, Michael didn't move.

Didn't breathe.

Didn't blink.

The smell of petrol.

Dust.

Hot metal.

Hassan's blood soaking through Michael's shirt.

A familiar coldness rose inside him – not shock, not grief, not yet. Something older. Something trained. Something that had been buried beneath years of trying to be a different kind of man.

A shadow he had promised himself he'd never let walk beside him again.

But now it stepped forward.

Slowly.

Deliberately.

He lowered Hassan gently to the ground and stood up.

The man in the back seat of the Land Cruiser stepped out, closing the door behind him with calm precision. He wasn't rushing. He wasn't fleeing. He wasn't trying to hide.

He was waiting.

Professional.

Controlled.

Umbra.

The man raised his pistol again, steady as a surgeon preparing a second incision.

Michael's voice came out low, shaped by something cold enough to burn.

"You shouldn't have done that."

The Umbra operator didn't answer – just fired.

Michael dropped behind the fuel barrel as the round punched through metal, spraying a thin mist of petrol into the air. He rolled to cover, grabbing a shard of broken concrete and hurling it to the left. The operator fired at the sound, shifting his position.

Michael lunged.

He closed the distance in a burst – fast, silent, lethal.

The Umbra man pivoted, blade already in hand, but Michael slammed into him, driving him back into the side of the vehicle. The pistol clattered to the ground. The knife swung upward – fast – but Michael caught the operator's wrist, twisting hard until tendons strained.

The man struck with his free elbow – sharp, brutal – catching Michael on the cheekbone. Pain flashed white.

Michael didn't stop.

He surged forward, smashing his forehead into the operator's nose. Cartilage cracked. Blood sprayed. The knife slipped free long enough for Michael to wrench the man's arm down and drive his knee into the elbow joint.

The snap was clean.

The scream wasn't.

The operator stumbled backward, clutching his ruined arm. Michael grabbed him by the collar and slammed him against the vehicle door.

"Who sent you?"

The operator spat blood into Michael's face.

Michael didn't react – he simply wiped it away with the back of his hand and pressed harder.

"Who. Sent. You?"

The man's eyes flickered – not with fear, but with the resignation of someone who knew death was already written into his orders.

"Redhawk," he whispered.

Michael froze.

"You're the reason," the operator continued, breath rattling. "You were always the reason."

Michael drove him back again. "Reason for what?"

"For all of it."

The words were barely audible – but Michael heard them.

Every syllable.

The man reached toward his chest – not for a weapon, but for a small device clipped beneath his vest.

A dead man's switch.

Michael wrenched it free, snapping the wire before the operator could engage it.

The man sagged, defeated. "Doesn't matter. They'll confirm. They always confirm."

Michael didn't hesitate.

He struck once, sharply, ending it.

Silence returned to the fuel station.

Real silence.

Heavy.

Settling over the dirt like ash.

Michael turned back to Hassan.

Kneeling beside his friend, he placed a hand over Hassan's heart – a gesture he had performed for too many men in too many countries, but it never landed any lighter.

"I'm sorry," he murmured.

It was not enough. It was all he had.

He closed Hassan's eyes and stood.

Across the road, two teenage boys who'd been drinking palm wine froze and then ran, disappearing between the houses. A woman who had been selling kola nuts crossed herself and backed away. The settlement absorbed the violence like dry ground absorbs rain – quickly, silently, without surprise.

Michael wiped the blood from his hands, his breath steady again.

He looked north.

If Umbra had killed Hassan here – in broad daylight, without camouflage or fear – then they were escalating.

No more surgical shadows.

No more hesitation.

They were sending messages now.

To him.

And to anyone who might stand beside him.

Michael walked toward the Land Cruiser, stepping over the dead operator. He opened the back door and scanned the interior.

Nothing unusual.

No documents.

No identification.

A standard Umbra clean vehicle.

But when he leaned forward to check the footwell, he saw it.

A small, etched metal disc.

Same design as the ring.

Serpent devouring its own tail.

But this one had a number engraved beneath it.

0091

A designation.

A unit marker.

A count.

Umbra did not make mistakes.

If they were assigning numbers, it meant they were tracking how many operators had been fed into the Redhawk assignment.

Michael pocketed the disc and stepped back into the sunlight.

Seven seconds passed before he heard the engine.

A Land Rover, olive green and dust-streaked, rolled into view from the upper road. A single man sat behind the wheel – older, broad-shouldered, wearing a faded shirt and an expression carved from stone.

He stopped the vehicle beside Michael.

The window rolled down.

"I think," the man said, voice level and unsettlingly calm, "you need to get in."

Michael didn't move. "Who are you?"

"That," the man said, "is an answer for the next ten minutes. Not this one."

Michael stared at him. "You armed?"

"Yes."

"You alone?"

"Yes."

"You Umbra?"

A pause – polite, almost respectful.

"No," the man said. "But we share an enemy."

Michael hesitated. Only for a heartbeat.

Then he opened the passenger door and got in.

The Land Rover pulled away from the fuel station, leaving the bodies – and Hassan's quiet, cooling form – behind.

As the settlement shrank in the rear-view mirror, Michael closed his eyes briefly.

Not in grief.

Not yet.

In promise.

Umbra had taken enough.

It was time they learned what it meant to hunt a man who refused to die on schedule.

The Land Rover rolled north, tyres humming over uneven tarmac and patches of red laterite. The air inside was warm, thick with dust and unsettled tension. Michael kept one hand braced against the door, the other resting near the handle of the machete strapped to his pack.

The driver said nothing for several minutes.

Michael broke the silence first.

"You knew Hassan."

The man nodded once. "Long enough to respect him. Not long enough to save him."

"Did you try?"

"I intercepted movement on the road," the man said. "Too late. They were already there."

Michael studied him more closely. The face was weathered – not from age, but from exposure. Sun-beaten African skin, scar beneath the left ear shaped like a crescent, eyes that held the quiet patience of someone who'd seen conflict from all sides and lived to understand every angle of it. Not military exactly. Not police. Something in between.

He didn't fit into a neat category.

Which meant he was dangerous.

"Name?" Michael asked.

"Adeyemi."

Nigerian.

Possibly Yoruba.

The accent was faint – educated, Continental, shaped by travel.

Michael nodded slowly. "Who are you working for?"

"Not Umbra," Adeyemi said. "Not the Consortium. Not any government you'd recognise."

"That's not a comforting answer."

"It wasn't meant to be."

He turned the steering wheel, guiding the Land Rover onto a long stretch of road that cut through abandoned farmland. Dry earth, scattered debris, half-built structures that had been swallowed by bush.

"We monitor movements," Adeyemi said finally. "Patterns. Groups. People who think the world forgets its own wounds." His grip tightened slightly on the steering wheel. "Umbra is not the only shadow. But it is the one growing fastest."

"And you monitor them."

"Someone must."

Michael's jaw tightened. "Hassan didn't deserve to die."

"No," Adeyemi agreed. "But he understood the stakes. He stayed too long. Watched too much."

Michael looked out the window, letting the countryside blur into colours.

"What did he find?" he asked.

"Evidence of movement between the coast and the interior. People. Supplies. Communications nodes that shouldn't exist." Adeyemi exhaled. "He thought you needed to know."

"And that's why Umbra killed him."

"No," Adeyemi said. "They killed him because he told the wrong person before he could tell you."

Michael turned sharply.

"Who?"

Adeyemi's silence lasted five beats too long.

"Vaughan," he said.

Michael closed his eyes briefly, feeling something inside him shift – not surprise, but confirmation.

Vaughan had pointed him toward Hassan.

Vaughan had known Umbra was close.

Vaughan had walked away from the settlement without fear of being followed.

"Why?" Michael asked quietly.

"Because Vaughan plays two sides against the third," Adeyemi said. "He survives by making sure someone else dies first."

Michael felt the heel of his palm press hard against his thigh, fighting down the instinct to turn back and hunt the man down immediately.

Adeyemi continued, "Vaughan didn't pull the trigger. But he lit the path to it."

The road dipped, curving toward a valley where mist clung between the trees like low smoke. Adeyemi slowed, shifting the Land Rover into a more cautious crawl.

"You said you monitor Umbra," Michael said. "Why come for me?"

"Because Hassan wasn't wrong," Adeyemi replied. "The things happening in Freetown, Port Loko, Samu – they're connected. The timing is not coincidence."

Michael leaned forward. "Connected how?"

Adeyemi looked at him, and for the first time the mask slipped enough for

Michael to see the concern beneath.

"They're preparing for something," Adeyemi said. "Not a coup. Not a resource grab. Something… coordinated. Umbra is only one limb of it."

Michael felt his heartbeat slow, not from calm, but calculation.

"Adeyemi," he said, "why do you care?"

The man stared ahead, eyes hardening.

"Because I've seen what happens when men with no allegiance build dreams with soldiers and money and silence." His voice dropped to almost a whisper. "I've seen what they leave behind."

Michael studied him. "Where are you taking me?"

"A safe position," Adeyemi said. "Temporary. Not permanent. You don't get permanence anymore." He glanced sideways. "No one in your orbit does."

Michael didn't argue. "And after that?"

"After that," Adeyemi said, "you decide what kind of witness you intend to be."

Michael frowned. "Witness to what?"

Adeyemi slowed the vehicle to a stop on a narrow ridge overlooking a vast spread of forest and lowland.

The engine idled.

The world around them went still.

Adeyemi pointed toward the horizon.

In the distance, faint but unmistakable, a line of trucks – unmarked, identical – crawled along a dirt track leading away from the coast.

A convoy.

A long one.

Too long to be coincidence.

Too coordinated to be smuggling.

Too quiet to be legitimate.

Michael felt the weight of it drop into place inside him.

"Umbra?" he asked.

"No," Adeyemi said. "Umbra is escort."

Michael inhaled slowly. "And the cargo?"

Adeyemi looked at him with the expression of a man who had already seen the answer.

"People," he said. "The kind who won't be seen again if you don't move soon."

Michael sat back, breath shallow, pulse steadying into something sharp, cold, and absolute.

He had been hunted.

He had been warned.

He had been pushed, prodded, and manoeuvred into the margins.

But now?

Now he could see the shape of what was happening.

Umbra wasn't just cleaning up.

They weren't chasing him.

They weren't reacting.

They were preparing.

Coordinating.

Building.

And he had just been shown the edge of the blueprint.

Adeyemi shifted into gear. "We don't have much time. Decide who you want to be."

Michael stared at the convoy disappearing into the trees – a line of steel, of stolen futures, moving under guard toward something none of them had the right to build.

When he spoke, his voice was low but carved from intent.

"I'm done being hunted."

He looked at Adeyemi.

"Take me to where this started."

Adeyemi nodded once.

"Then hold on."

The Land Rover lurched forward, tyres spitting dust into the rising heat as they tore down the ridge.

The hunt had changed direction.

Michael wasn't running anymore.

Now he was coming.

CHAPTER 8

THE THIN LINE OF SILENCE

"A secret that walks in daylight is already choosing its witness."
– AFRICAN PROVERB

Dawn broke hard over Conakry, a flat, colourless light that made the edges of every building look brittle. The city hadn't woken yet, not properly – the early markets were only just beginning to murmur, and the mosquito buzz of motorcycle taxis was still scattered and uncertain. Michael walked with purpose, hood up, collar raised, moving through alleys he knew better than any official map ever could.

He needed to be alone before anyone could decide he shouldn't be.

The warehouse wasn't on any registry. A forgotten block on an old shipping ledger, left to rot between a disused fish-processing plant and a mechanic's yard that no longer repaired anything. He slipped inside through a gap in the corrugated sheet metal, letting the darkness swallow him whole.

Inside, dust hung low in the air, caught in a single shaft of pale light filtering through a tear in the roof. The room smelled of stale salt, oil, and the memory of cargo long gone. On a raised platform at the back stood a man waiting for him – broad-shouldered, gold tooth catching the faint light, face lined with years of knowing too much.

He didn't turn immediately. "You took your time."

"I had company on the road," Michael said.

The man gave a small approving grunt. "If they'd wanted you dead, they'd have sent a drone. Or poison. Bullets are for the noisy parts of a story."

"Who are you working for?" Michael asked.

The man finally faced him. "People who don't like unfinished business," he said. "And you, Michael Sillah, are unfinished business."

He reached into a battered folder and pulled out a sheaf of satellite images. Not copies – originals. Classified format. Crisp resolution. Something that had bypassed the usual channels.

He spread them on an old crate.

Road patterns.

Heat signatures.

Movement trails.

A faint, unmistakable outline of a developing perimeter.

"Where did you get these?" Michael asked.

"Same place everyone gets forbidden things," the man said. "A place with no flag, no anthem, and a very long memory."

Michael leaned closer. The images weren't of Samu itself – not directly – but of the approaches around it, the paths he'd taken only a day before. They showed tyre tracks, footpaths cleared through brush, small structures that hadn't existed six months ago. It was a logistical spine, half-finished and half-hidden.

"Someone's building something," Michael murmured.

The man nodded. "Someone always is. The trick is knowing whether it's a wall, a road, or a cage."

He slid one more image across. It had been folded separately, edges creased by a rough hand.

A message written in black marker ink along the bottom:

Samu is active. The watchers are not alone.

Michael's pulse tightened. Not with fear – but recognition.

"Who wrote this?" he asked.

"Someone who thought you should know," the man replied. "Someone who won't be alive much longer."

Michael absorbed that quietly.

The man studied him for a moment. "You came back here for a reason."

"I had to confirm something."

"And did you?"

Michael looked at the images again – the tracks, the shadows, the angles.

"Yes."

He slid the last image back across the crate.

"I'm not the one being hunted," he said. "I'm the one being positioned."

The man's gold tooth glinted. "Then the game's further along than I thought."

Michael straightened. "Why tell me any of this?"

"Because Samu is older than you think," the man said. "Older than this government. Older than the wars. And men with rings and clean boots don't go there unless someone with money tells them exactly where to stand."

Michael stepped back toward the exit. "You said people sent you."

"They did."

"What do they want from me?"

The man smiled – a slow, tired expression lacking any humour.

"To keep breathing," he said. "At least until the right moment."

"And after that?"

The smile disappeared. "After that, I'd advise running."

Michael left the warehouse before the man could say anything else. The city's heat met him like an accusation, heavy and immediate. The alleys felt narrower, the buildings taller, the sky lower. Conakry had always been a city of divided loyalties, but today it felt like it was holding its breath.

He made it halfway down the block before he sensed the shift – that faint prickle between the shoulder blades that told him he was no longer just being watched.

He was being shepherded.

Toward what, he didn't yet know.

But whatever it was, Samu had not been the beginning.

It had been the opening door.

And something was waiting on the other side.

The city's pulse thickened as Michael moved through it – traffic grinding awake, street vendors shouting prices, the scent of frying akara mixing with diesel fumes and something sharp and metallic. Conakry had a habit of swallowing secrets, but today it felt like secrets were moving faster than the people carrying them.

He crossed the main road and slipped into a courtyard behind a seamstress's shop. Three young men clustered there, smoking and pretending to play draughts. One of them glanced up, recognition flickering before he looked away. Safe enough.

Michael kept moving.

He reached the small bakery at the corner of Rue de Niger – a place he and Tamba had used for quiet meetings long before the country's politics began curdling again. The woman behind the counter kneaded dough with vigorous, angry efficiency, but when she caught sight of him, her expression softened just slightly.

"You're late," she said without looking up.

Michael nodded. "I'm aware."

"Tamba is at the back. He didn't sleep."

Michael moved through the narrow corridor to the loading area, where the air was thick with the smell of warm bread and stove ash. Tamba sat on an upturned crate, elbows on knees, gaze fixed on the floor.

He looked up when Michael approached, and for a moment – a rare, fragile moment – he looked like the younger man Michael had once trained: sharp, fierce, but still capable of hope.

"You look tired," Michael said quietly.

Tamba exhaled. "I've seen too much in two days."

"Any of it good?"

"No."

Michael sat beside him. Silence settled between them, heavy but not hostile.

"I had visitors," Tamba said. "Two men in a Hilux. They weren't local. They weren't trying to hide it."

"Umbra?"

"I don't know. But they asked about you." He ran a hand across his face. "And about Samu."

The air between them tightened.

"What did you tell them?" Michael asked.

"That I hadn't seen you in months," Tamba replied. "And that Samu was a graveyard – nothing more."

Michael nodded slowly. "Thank you."

"Don't thank me yet," Tamba said. "They were looking for something. Someone. And they weren't shy about letting people know they had authority. The kind of authority no one argues with because no one knows who gave it."

Michael leaned back. "What else?"

Tamba hesitated. "Trucks moved through the port last night. Late. Quiet. No manifests. No usual officers. The kind of operation that makes even corrupt men nervous."

"Where were they headed?"

"Interior."

"Coast to inland. Umbra patterns," Michael muttered.

Tamba frowned. "Umbra's too big a name for what this felt like."

"What did it feel like?"

Tamba looked at him – really looked.

"State," he said. "But not our state."

Michael absorbed that.

Tamba continued, voice low. "And I heard something else. A rumour only. That a foreign adviser had returned to the country." He lifted an eyebrow. "A ghost from the coup days, they said."

Michael kept his face still. "Rumours are cheap."

"Not these ones," Tamba said. "They came from people who don't traffic in chatter. People who watch. People who wait."

Michael felt something tighten in his chest. "Gibril?"

Tamba didn't answer. He didn't have to.

"Why now?" Michael murmured.

"Why anything now?" Tamba countered. "Your name's been in rooms it shouldn't be. And Gibril… he's not the sort of man who reappears without a reason."

Michael breathed out slowly. "There's pressure building."

"There's more than pressure," Tamba said. "Something is aligning. People are moving who shouldn't. Money is flowing where it's never flowed. And the men who know how to read the wind – they're keeping their children indoors."

Michael rubbed his hands together, grounding his thoughts. "I need to see something."

"What?"

"There was an envelope," Michael said. "Before Samu. Now there's another."

He reached into his pocket and produced the envelope he'd been given earlier that morning – not the one from the warehouse, but a different one entirely, crudely sealed, smudged with oil.

Tamba frowned. "Another message?"

Michael tore it open.

Inside was a single line, written in the same ink-black hand as before:

Do not go to Samu.

Tamba looked at him. "Someone's protecting you."

"Or trying to steer me."

"Toward what?"

Michael exhaled. "Toward either truth… or a trap. Hard to know which without stepping on the pressure plate."

"You going back?"

"No," Michael said, folding the message. "Not yet."

He pocketed the note and stood.

Tamba rose with him. “You’re being pulled into something deep, Michael. You know that.”

“I don’t have a choice.”

“You always have a choice,” Tamba said. “But you stopped wanting one a long time ago.”

Michael allowed himself the faintest of smiles. “Maybe.”

Tamba placed a hand on Michael’s shoulder – a gesture of trust, warning, and resignation all at once. “Be careful. Everyone’s playing angles. I don’t know who’s on your side.”

“Neither do I,” Michael said. “Which is why I’m still alive.”

He stepped out of the bakery and back into the rising heat, the city shifting around him with the restless energy of a place bracing for something it could feel but not name.

Conakry wasn’t just holding its breath anymore.

It was listening.

Michael followed the spine of the city north, weaving between market carts and the early swell of minibuses grinding toward the centre. The noise rose, but his thoughts stayed sharp, cutting through the static.

The second envelope had changed things.

Two messages.

Two warnings.

Two hands pulling him in opposite directions.

Someone wanted him near Samu.

Someone else wanted him far from it.

Neither wanted him dead – at least not yet.

That meant he was useful.

Or dangerous.

Or both.

He walked until the city thinned and the dust roads widened into the open scars of development projects long abandoned. A half-constructed tower block loomed overhead, its concrete skeleton exposed to the heat like the ribs of a fallen animal.

This had once been the Government’s pride – a planned expansion, foreign investment, a symbol of progress.

Then politics shifted.

Money vanished.

And the project died in the sun.

Now it served another purpose.

He slipped into the shell of the structure, boots echoing across the hollow floors. The air was heavy, dense with humidity and the smell of old cement. He made for the eastern side, where he could see the curve of the coastline and, beyond it, the vague outline of the forested interior that led toward Samu.

He stopped at a broken window frame, anchoring his hands on the concrete as if balancing himself on a thought too sharp to hold freely.

Samu.

The name wasn't just a place.

It was a fault line.

Every time he'd returned to that part of his past, something had shifted – people had died, secrets had surfaced, shadows had lengthened. Mariama's voice drifted through him in fragments, unbidden: warnings, laughter, the soft cadence of her breath when she slept.

The dead do not stay quiet, Michael.

They wait.

They watch.

And they deserve witnesses.

He closed his eyes briefly.

The ache hadn't faded.

Not since he left Sierra Leone the first time.

Not since he tried to outrun the coup and everything it had corrupted.

He opened them again to the sound of a soft scrape behind him.

He turned.

A young boy stood at the entrance to the level – barefoot, cautious, carrying a plastic bottle of water. He looked at Michael with uncertain curiosity.

"You are the man looking for the old camp," the boy said.

Michael kept his voice low. "Who told you that?"

The boy pointed toward the street below. "The woman with the scarf. She said to come tell you not to go alone."

Michael stiffened. "What woman?"

"Tall. Quiet. Eyes like she is counting things."

Fatmata.

He exhaled slowly. "Where did she go?"

"She said she would meet you if you keep walking east."

He handed Michael the bottle and darted away, disappearing down the crumbling stairwell like a shadow slipping through cracks.

Michael unscrewed the cap, took a slow drink, then set the bottle down.

Fatmata had been careful before. Too careful to leave open messages. If she was resurfacing now, it meant she had seen something she didn't want to say aloud.

He left the ruin and followed the eastern road.

Twenty minutes later, he found her.

She stood beneath an outcropping of almond trees, half-hidden in their shade, a dusty shawl drawn over her head. Her posture was easy, but her eyes were alert – scanning constantly, mapping the angles.

"Busy morning," she said.

"You followed me."

"Yes."

"Why?"

Fatmata stepped forward. "Because the men who kill in daylight don't care who sees them anymore. And because you, Michael, leave a trail even when you think you're walking in silence."

"What did you hear?"

"Whispers." She glanced toward the road. "And news from the checkpoints."

"What news?"

She hesitated – then spoke.

"They are looking for someone with your build. Not your name. Not your face. Just the build. The way you move. The way you carry weight on your left side." Her voice softened. "Someone has described you to people who don't use names."

Michael inhaled once through his nose. "Umbra?"

"Umbra… and others." Fatmata's jaw tightened. "People from Freetown. People not in uniform."

"State?"

"State-adjacent," she said. "Like they answer to a ministry no one visits."

Michael folded his arms. "What else?"

"A convoy left the airport last night," she said. "Large. Not UN. Not police. Escorts wearing boots too clean for this heat."

Michael frowned. "Destination?"

"Interior," she said. "Same pattern as the trucks your friend Hassan saw."

A sharp pulse of grief flickered behind his sternum – gone almost instantly.

Fatmata watched him. "You're angry."

"I'm focused."

She nodded slowly. "Good. But don't be alone in that focus. It will make you predictable."

They walked together for a few paces until the trees thinned and the road widened.

Fatmata stopped.

"There is something else," she said quietly.

Michael waited.

"People have seen your old friend," she murmured. "The one from the coup days. The one who vanished."

Michael felt the world narrow beneath his feet.

"Gibril?" he asked.

She nodded. "He passed through Conakry. Not openly. But people saw enough."

"Doing what?"

"Meeting someone," she said. "A woman with a diplomatic passport. And a man with a briefcase that didn't match his clothes."

Michael looked away toward the interior – the long stretch of land between here and Samu, and whatever ghosts walked between them.

"He's coming back into the story," Michael said.

"He never left," Fatmata replied. "He just changed chapters."

A silence settled between them – loaded, brittle, waiting to crack.

Fatmata adjusted her scarf. "You're going to go after the next thread," she said simply. "You always do."

Michael met her eyes. "Do you know where he went?"

She nodded once. "Toward the coast. Toward someone with money. Toward someone who thinks men like him are useful again."

Michael exhaled, slow and steady.

"And you're going to follow that thread," she said.

"Yes."

Fatmata looked at him for a long moment. "Then be careful. There are hands moving pieces you don't see yet."

"And you?"

"I'll stay in the shade," she said. "And listen to the parts you can't hear."

He almost smiled. Almost.

Then he walked east again, toward the coastline, toward the next link in the chain.

Each step was a quiet oath.

Hassan had died for this.

Samu had awakened for this.

Gibril had resurfaced for this.

And the shadows between them were beginning to converge.

The coastline road curved like a fractured spine, running parallel to the Atlantic where waves struck the rocks in slow, rhythmic blows. The sky had shifted to a washed-out grey, the kind that preceded either rain or revelation.

Michael kept moving.

He passed fishermen repairing torn nets, women carrying buckets of water balanced on cloth-wrapped heads, clusters of children playing football with bound-twine balls. Life continued as if nothing beneath it was rearranging itself.

But Michael felt the shift – the subtle tightening in the air, like an unseen hand pulling a thread through layers of fabric.

Ahead, a battered roadside café sat crookedly at the edge of the cliff, looking as though the sea had tried to claim it several times and grown bored. A generator rattled weakly beside it.

He stepped inside.

The woman behind the counter barely looked up. She was tall, wrapped in a faded indigo cloth that had once carried brighter patterns. Her expression was unreadable – neither welcoming nor suspicious, simply observant.

"You're late," she said.

Michael studied her. "Do I know you?"

"You don't," she replied. "But others do."

She wiped a glass that didn't need wiping. "He left something for you."

"Who?"

She slid a small envelope from beneath the counter. Unmarked. Weathered. Hand-delivered.

"He said you'd come alone."

Michael opened it.

A single line, written in tight, restrained handwriting:

They're moving faster than you think. Do not trust the man with the walking cane.

Michael inhaled once. Slowly.

Vaughan.

Of course.

The woman watched him closely. "Bad news?"

"Expected news."

He folded the note. "Did he say anything else?"

She considered for a moment. "He said you were running out of time."

Michael pocketed the envelope. "Which direction?"

The woman nodded toward the cliff path leading southwest, tracing the coastline. "He went that way. With someone he shouldn't have been seen with."

"Who?"

"White blazer. Senegalese plates. The kind of car that drives through checkpoints without slowing."

Michael felt the first spark of anticipation – sharp, cold, clarifying.

Diplomatic cover.

Regional connections.

A convenient cloak for inconvenient deals.

"Thank you," he said.

The woman gave a dry smile. "Men like him don't survive long. Men like you survive longer. Usually."

He stepped outside.

The air had thickened with salt and storm promise. He followed the cliff path, boots crunching over loose stones. The coastline widened into a plateau overlooking the sea. A series of concrete bunkers sat abandoned nearby – relics of old military programmes forgotten by everyone except the people who had once died defending them.

He slowed.

A sound drifted from inside one of the bunkers – a faint hum, like electricity running where no generator should be.

He approached the entrance, adjusting his stance, weight low, every sense narrowing to a point.

Inside, dim light flickered from a single battery lamp hung on a hook. A makeshift table held papers weighed down by stones. Tracks in the dust showed recent movement – someone had been here only minutes before.

On the floor lay something that stopped him cold.

A photograph.

Face-down.

He picked it up.

Mariama.

Her smile captured in the soft light of a long-ago evening. The photo wasn't old – not faded, not torn. It had been reprinted recently.

His fingers tightened around it.

This wasn't an accident.

Not a coincidence.

Not a message left without intent.

Someone was threading her memory into this operation with surgical precision.

He turned the photograph over.

On the back, written in neat, deliberate handwriting:

You were never meant to leave Sierra Leone.

– G.S.

Gibril Sillah.

His cousin.

His ghost.

His unfinished war.

Michael exhaled slowly – not shock, not grief, but an anchored certainty.

Gibril was close.

Watching.

Pulling strings from behind the curtain.

And the re-emergence of Mariama's image was not just a warning.

It was an invitation.

Footsteps echoed at the bunker's entrance – heavy, deliberate, approaching.

Michael pivoted silently, sliding into the shadows.

A man stepped inside.

Tall. Lean. Wearing a diplomatic lanyard tucked discreetly under his shirt. His posture was the kind of confident that came from being protected by letters of immunity and the belief that consequences were optional.

He stopped at the table, scanning the papers.

Michael moved before the man could turn.

He grabbed him by the collar, slammed him against the bunker wall, and pinned him there with an arm across his throat.

"Where is Gibril?" Michael demanded.

The diplomat's eyes widened. "I–I don't know–"

Michael pressed harder. "Wrong answer."

"I only passed a message!" the man gasped. "That's all!"

"What message?"

"That you would come," the man stammered. "And that he would be ready."

Michael's jaw tightened. "Ready for what?"

The diplomat swallowed hard, eyes darting toward the photograph on the floor.

"For the reckoning," he whispered.

A cold stillness settled over the bunker.

Michael released him abruptly. The man collapsed to the ground, coughing and scrambling away like a startled animal.

"Go," Michael said.

The man didn't need to be told twice.

He bolted down the cliff path, stumbling in his panic, disappearing into the salt haze.

Michael picked up the photograph again, running his thumb along the edge. Mariama's smile felt like a blade being lovingly sharpened.

The sea crashed against the rocks below, each wave striking like a distant heartbeat.

He slipped the photograph into his jacket.

Gibril had made his move.

And Michael was done absorbing the blows.

It was time to return them.

He stepped out of the bunker, into the rising wind, the horizon darkening ahead – storm clouds gathering over the interior, the direction of Samu, of the convoys, of the shadows tightening their circle.

Michael breathed once, deeply.

Then he walked.

Not away.

Not toward safety.

But directly into the next fracture line of the world being built behind closed doors.

He didn't intend to be its witness anymore.

He intended to be its interruption.

Chapter 9

FIRE ON THE TARMAC

"When the storm cannot find you,
it persuades others to lead you into its path."
– African proverb

Night had thinned into a bruised, early light over the airport perimeter, the kind that made every edge look sharpened, every shadow longer than it should be. The air smelled of hot rubber, old jet fuel and the metallic taste of anticipation. Michael moved in low along the fence line, Seray and Alhaji at his flanks, all three keeping to the broken patches of scrub that skirted the outer access road.

They had been running since the river – north, then west, then back south again – using goat tracks and abandoned construction sites to throw off the men who were hunting them. Now they were approaching a place that should have been loud, bustling, alive.

Instead, the airport felt like a vacuum.

Too quiet.

Too still.

Too expectant.

Seray noticed it at the same time he did. "Where's the ground crew?" she whispered.

"Shift change?" Alhaji offered.

Michael shook his head. "Not all at once. Not here."

He scanned the eastern tarmac. Floodlights were still on, humming faintly, but there was no movement beneath them – no handlers, no carts, no early arrivals. Just a single line of shipping containers stacked neatly near the decommissioned service hangar.

Three guards patrolled the line.

Not airport security.

Not police.

Umbra.

Michael gestured for the others to stay low as they crept closer through a gully choked with dry grass and discarded tyres. A faint clatter echoed from the far side of the container row – quick, metallic, too light to be machinery.

Seray froze. "Movement. Small. Could be animal."

Michael shook his head again. "Animals don't check sightlines."

He risked a glance through a rusted break in the fence.

A tall man stepped into view. Slender. White shirt rolled to the elbows. A black cane tapping lightly against concrete as he walked toward the guards.

Michael exhaled once through his teeth.

Vaughan.

Seray leaned close. "Your friend?"

"No," Michael said quietly. "Not anymore."

Vaughan exchanged a few low words with the guards, then tapped the cane twice against the nearest container. One of the men unlocked it.

A slow groaning sound followed as the door slid open.

Seray sucked in a breath. "Holy–"

Inside the container, illuminated by the spill of floodlight, was a painted symbol: a rising phoenix, wings outstretched, layered over black and crimson geometric lines.

Michael felt the recognition hit like a tightening band around his ribs.

"Consortium," he whispered.

The same symbol from the inland base.

The same symbol in the Samu shadows.

The same symbol Hassan had died trying to expose.

Vaughan lifted a folder from inside the container, flicked it open, skimmed the contents, then closed it again with a thoughtful, almost satisfied gesture.

He tapped the cane lightly and said something Michael couldn't hear, but whatever it was sent the guards into motion. They began inspecting the other containers, one after another.

Alhaji tensed beside him. "What are they doing?"

"Inventory," Michael murmured. "Checking the shipment before it moves."

"Moves where?" Seray asked.

Michael's jaw clenched. "Interior. Always interior."

Vaughan suddenly paused. He looked up, scanning the horizon as though drawn by a thread. Not in their direction exactly – but close enough that Michael felt the hairs on his arms rise.

Seray whispered, "He senses something."

Michael nodded. "He always did."

Vaughan turned away and snapped his fingers toward the guards. They followed him toward a waiting Hilux marked with diplomatic plates.

Seray blinked. "Since when does Umbra use diplomatic cover?"

"Since someone paid for it," Michael said.

"You think that… thing they're working with is state-level?"

Michael looked again at the phoenix symbol burning like a quiet threat inside the open container.

"No," he said. "I think it's above state-level."

The Hilux engine revved.

Michael's pulse tightened.

They had seconds before Vaughan left their reach.

He touched Seray's shoulder. "We move now. Quiet but fast."

"Into the open?" she whispered.

"Into the opportunity," he replied.

The three of them ghosted along the gully, slipping through a break in the fence and into the shadow line of the hangar. Michael signalled left. Alhaji peeled off to maintain a flank position. Seray matched Michael stride for stride.

The Hilux rolled slowly forward, headlights still off.

One guard lagged behind to secure the containers.

Michael angled toward him.

Three steps.

Two.

One–

The guard turned and saw him.

Too late.

Michael struck first – elbow to throat, knife-hand to wrist, dropping the man before he could raise his weapon. Seray dragged the body into the shadow of the hangar wall.

The Hilux slowed, as though Vaughan sensed a shift in the air but didn't yet know its shape.

"Now," Michael breathed.

He sprinted toward the service stairwell that led up to the abandoned emergency observation deck – the only vantage point that would let them see the entire container array and whatever Vaughan did next.

Seray followed.

Below them, Vaughan stepped out of the Hilux and tapped his cane twice – the signal he'd used in Istanbul years before, when he'd been on their side of the line.

Michael swallowed a spark of old bitterness.

The man they were about to confront had once saved his life.

And maybe ruined it.

He reached the top of the stairs, pushed open the observation door –

And froze.

Inside, sitting on a metal chair in the half-light, was a man whose silhouette he recognised long before the face came into view.

Orion.

The mentor who had vanished.

The traitor Michael had once defended.

The architect of a dozen quiet disasters.

He was waiting.

As though he had expected Michael at this exact moment, on this exact stairwell, in this exact forgotten corner of the airport.

"Hello, Michael," Orion said without standing. "You're late."

Orion didn't move. Didn't blink. Just rested both hands on the head of an old walking stick – not elegant like Vaughan's cane, but worn smooth by years of use. His face was leaner than Michael remembered; cheekbones sharper, hair shot with more grey, eyes colder but clearer. A man whittled down, not weakened.

Seray stepped in beside Michael, gun already half raised.

Orion smirked. "If you were going to shoot me, you would have done it before you opened the door. That hesitation, Michael… you really are getting slower."

Michael didn't rise to it. "Why are you here?"

"Because Vaughan wanted an audience," Orion said lightly. "And because you have a habit of arriving where the story turns."

Seray moved forward. "Try another word and you'll be chewing your own teeth."

Orion's grin widened. "Ah. The feisty one. I like you."

Michael stepped between them. "Talk."

"I will," Orion said. "But understand this first: you're standing in the middle of something vast. Something that didn't begin at Samu, or with the coup, or with Mariama. This game has been running beneath you for years. You've only just noticed the ripples."

Michael's jaw tightened. "You left men to die in Dakar."

"I left everyone to die in Dakar," Orion corrected. "Including myself. But some of us are inconveniently hard to kill."

Michael glanced through the dusty glass windows toward the tarmac. Vaughan was still inspecting the containers, the phoenix symbol half-visible in the floodlight glow.

"Tell me about the Consortium," Michael said.

Orion's eyebrow lifted. "You already know enough."

"Not from you."

A flicker – the first crack in Orion's composure. "The Consortium is older than Umbra. Older than the governments pretending to run this region. They're an economic hydra with military taste. They don't believe in borders. They believe in outcomes."

"And the phoenix?" Seray asked.

Orion nodded approvingly. "Good question. The phoenix isn't a logo. It's a promise. Each branch of the network… rises from the ashes of the one that fails. A built-in resurrection clause. Failures aren't punished – they're simply… repurposed."

Michael folded his arms. "And what do they want here?"

"Control," Orion said. "Control of transit lanes. Control of mineral routes. Control of people." He leaned forward. "Sierra Leone is a pivot point, Michael. Always has been. For centuries. You think they're the first to see it?"

"Why the airport?"

"Because airports move the world faster than borders do," Orion said. "And because no one checks the containers marked for humanitarian transit anymore. People assume the suffering is already inside."

Michael felt a familiar coldness settle at the base of his spine. "You were part of this."

"Not willingly," Orion said. "Not fully. But once you've been inside a machine like that, it's very hard to step outside and pretend you're clean."

Seray stepped to the far window, scanning lower levels. "Movement. More guards coming in."

Orion sighed. "That's the problem with conversations like this. They never last long."

Michael stepped closer. "Why warn me? Why now?"

"Because you're the only one stupid enough to get in their way and stubborn enough to keep going," Orion said. "And because Gibril respects you."

Michael froze.

Orion's smile sharpened. "Ah. There it is. Yes, he knows you're alive. Yes, he's closer than you think. And yes, he's working with them – but not fully. Gibril plays his own games."

Michael kept his voice steady. "Where is he?"

"You'll see him when he wants to be seen," Orion said. "But don't confuse his interest for loyalty. Mariama taught you better than that."

The name hit like a pressure point.

Seray shot Orion a daggered glare. "You don't get to use her name."

Orion lifted a hand. "Fair. But she's part of this too. Her death wasn't an accident. You know that."

A quiet rupture opened in the air – invisible, but felt.

Michael's voice dropped. "Walk very carefully with that sentence."

Orion leaned back, fully aware of the danger. "The truth is a weapon. I'm simply returning yours."

Footsteps echoed outside the observation deck – boots, multiple sets, closing in.

Seray hissed, "We're out of time."

Michael grabbed Orion by the shirt and pulled him upright. "If you betray me again–"

"I won't," Orion said simply. "Because you're the only leverage I have left."

Michael shoved him toward the door. "Move."

Orion limped down the stairwell quicker than expected, still agile despite the limp, Seray covering the rear. Michael judged distances, counted shadows, listened to the cadence of the approaching squad.

Umbra. And armed.

They hit the bottom step as the first burst of gunfire tore through the metal siding behind them.

Seray shoved Orion behind a support pillar. "Stay low!"

Orion barked a laugh. "I'm not an idiot–"

A second burst cut him off, and Michael dragged Seray right, rolling behind stacked cargo pallets.

Alhaji's voice crackled faintly through their comm unit. "Company incoming. Three vehicles. Tactical pattern."

"We see them," Michael murmured.

Seray chambered a round. "What now?"

Michael looked toward the tarmac – toward Vaughan's Hilux beginning to roll forward, toward the containers, toward the phoenix rising in painted silence.

"Now," Michael said, "we take the fight outside."

He pulled a flash grenade from his belt.

Seray grinned. "Finally."

They burst from cover and entered the storm.

The flash grenade detonated with a crack of white fire, light blooming across the hangar's metal skin. The Umbra squad staggered, vision blown open, guns firing blind in panicked bursts. Michael and Seray were already moving – low, fast, cutting across the open ground toward the shadow of the abandoned fuel truck.

Alhaji emerged from the far side, rifle braced, muzzle dropping two stunned operators before they could recover.

"Left flank!" he shouted.

Michael pivoted, firing a tight controlled pair into the closest target. The Umbra man dropped to his knees, helmet clattering against the tarmac. The Hilux carrying Vaughan began accelerating away from the container line, tyres screaming as it fishtailed across the open space.

"Seray!" Michael barked.

She understood instantly.

She sprinted toward the rising service ramp that led to the maintenance scaffolding above the tarmac. From up there she would have a clean angle on Vaughan's fleeing vehicle.

Michael didn't watch her climb – he trusted her implicitly. Instead, he pushed toward the container array with Alhaji at his flank. Another Umbra operator rounded the corner, weapon raised, but Michael slammed into him before he could fire, grabbing the barrel, twisting, using the man's momentum to throw him into the steel wall of the container.

The operator's skull cracked against metal.

He didn't get back up.

Alhaji stopped beside him, breathing hard. "They're pushing toward the runway!"

"Good," Michael said. "We follow."

But before they could move, something caught Michael's eye – a thin trail of dust rising behind the container with the phoenix emblem. A barely perceptible disturbance on the ground. Recent.

A sliding track.

A hidden access panel.

He dropped into a crouch.

"Alhaji – here."

Together they shoved the heavy container aside just enough to reveal a secondary hatch built into the concrete floor. Not airport construction – the hinges were new, camouflaged beneath grit.

Someone had installed this recently. Someone with clearance. Someone with money.

Michael pulled the hatch open.

Cool air rushed upward, tinged with diesel, sweat, and something metallic – like old blood and new fear.

A service tunnel.

But not an official one.

Alhaji swallowed. "This wasn't in the plans."

"It wasn't meant to be," Michael murmured. "It's how they're moving whatever they don't want seen."

He lowered himself into the tunnel. The walls were reinforced. New wiring ran along the ceiling. Footprints in the dust. Two sets. One heavy, one lighter. One dragging slightly – someone injured or being forced.

Seray's voice crackled in his earpiece. "I've got eyes on Vaughan. He's heading for the runway taxi lane. You have sixty seconds before he's gone."

Michael's pulse hardened. "Stay tracking. Don't engage alone."

"Not planning to," she said. "But I'm not letting him vanish."

Michael hesitated – tunnel or Vaughan?

He made the decision in one breath.

"Alhaji – follow Vaughan. Support Seray."

"You sure?"

"Yes."

Alhaji nodded once and sprinted after Seray's position.

Michael turned back into the tunnel, weapon raised.

The darkness felt alive.

He moved deeper, following the footprints, ears tuned to every shift in the air. The tunnel sloped downward, then levelled out, then opened into a wider chamber lit by a single generator-powered lamp.

That's when he saw it.

A line of cages.

Six of them.

Reinforced. Locked.

Five empty.

One occupied.

A man slumped against the bars, hands shackled, head bowed. His clothes were torn, caked with dust. His breath shallow, ragged.

Michael approached slowly.

As he came close, the man lifted his head.

Michael froze.

It was the driver from the Kambia checkpoint – the one who had turned him away two nights ago with careful, unspoken warning in his eyes.

He was barely conscious.

Recognition flickered. "S… Sillah," the man whispered, voice cracked. "They… they knew you'd return."

Michael crouched beside him, gripping the bars. "Who brought you here?"

The man coughed, wincing. "Operators… some Umbra, some not. They… they asked about the coin."

Michael's breath caught. "What coin?"

"The one… you dropped," the man whispered. "At the checkpoint. They said… it meant you were marked."

Michael felt the cold thread of fate tighten against his spine.

The coin.

The ouroboros symbol.

Umbra's internal tally system.

"Who used it?" Michael asked. "Who knows what it means?"

The man's eyes fluttered. "The one… with the walk… the one who never shows his face… Red–"

A burst of gunfire exploded behind Michael.

He spun.

Two figures had entered the chamber – one Umbra, one wearing civilian clothes with a tactical vest and a headset.

The civilian spoke first.

"Michael Sillah. Finally."

The voice was modulated – artificial.

Michael fired.

The first man dropped instantly. The second ducked behind the generator, returning fire that ricocheted off steel and concrete.

Michael rolled behind a cage, bullets chewing into the walls around him. The generator sparked violently as rounds clipped it, throwing half the chamber into jerking shadows.

"Do you even know why you're still alive?" the modulated voice taunted.

Michael stayed low. "Enlighten me."

"You're leverage," the voice replied. "Nothing more. Nothing less."

Michael fired three blind shots toward the voice's source and moved right.

"I've been watching you since Freetown. Since Samu. Since Mariama."

Michael froze.

The voice smiled inside its distortion. "Ah. Sensitive spot."

Michael rose, sweeping left, firing –

Silence.

The attacker was gone.

A secondary tunnel entrance stood open behind the generator – a narrow slit of darkness leading deeper underground.

Michael cursed once under his breath.

He sprinted back to the cage, found the latch, and smashed it open with the butt of his rifle. He pulled the injured man out and slung him over his shoulder.

"Stay with me," Michael said. "You're not dying here."

Above him, faint through the concrete, he heard the distant roar of an engine accelerating hard –

Vaughan's Hilux.

Seray's voice burst through the comms, strained, breathless.

"Michael–he's heading for the outer barrier. If he breaches it, he's gone into open ground!"

Michael climbed the tunnel ladder, hauling the survivor with him.

Halfway up, he whispered to himself:

"Not today."

He pushed through the hatch –

And emerged into the chaos.

Michael hit the surface with the injured man over his shoulder just as the tarmac erupted into motion.

Two Umbra operators were sprinting toward Vaughan's Hilux, weapons raised. Seray was on the scaffolding above them, firing disciplined, precise bursts that forced the operators to scatter for cover. Alhaji was pinned down behind a luggage cart, returning fire in controlled arcs that kept the squad from closing in.

The Hilux was already thirty metres ahead and accelerating.

Vaughan leaned out of the passenger window long enough to look back – not with fear, but with smug appraisal, like a man checking the time before catching a train he already knew would leave on schedule.

Michael lowered the injured man behind cover. "Stay down!"

He ran.

His boots hammered against the cracked concrete, breath pushing past the burn in his chest. One Umbra operator rose to intercept him – Michael struck hard, slamming the man's wrist against a fuel drum, knocking the rifle free, then driving a knee into his ribs until he collapsed.

"Seray!" he shouted.

"Tracking him!" she called back. "Take the service lane–he's boxed in!"

Michael vaulted a baggage conveyor, cutting across the dead space between the hangar and the outer barrier. He could see the Hilux fighting for speed – tyres spitting gravel as it tried to gain the straightaway that led toward the perimeter gate.

Vaughan was escaping.

Not today. Not again.

Another Umbra operator came at him from the left, but before Michael could react, Alhaji dropped the man with a clean headshot.

"Go!" Alhaji yelled. "We'll hold the line!"

Michael pushed harder, legs screaming, lungs burning. The Hilux roared, fishtailing as Vaughan shouted something at the driver. They were almost at the barrier now – a flimsy metal gate flanked by concrete blocks designed to keep livestock out, not ghosts like Vaughan in.

Seray shifted position, climbing higher onto the scaffolding. She steadied her rifle.

"I've got the tyres," she said.

"Do it!" Michael barked.

She fired twice.

The rounds struck the Hilux's rear wheel – perfect hits – shredding the rubber and sending the vehicle skidding sideways. It spun in a violent arc, metal shrieking across concrete, and slammed into the barrier.

Michael didn't slow.

He reached the vehicle just as Vaughan kicked the door open and staggered out, dust and smoke curling around him. His cane clattered to the ground. For the first time in years, Vaughan looked genuinely off balance.

He saw Michael.

And smiled.

"You're faster than the reports suggested," Vaughan said, breathless.

Michael didn't respond. He closed the distance, grabbing Vaughan by the collar and slamming him hard against the wrecked door.

"Why the containers?" Michael demanded. "Why the phoenix? Why now?"

Vaughan laughed – a tired, broken sound. "Because the world is being rearranged, my friend. And you're one of the pieces that never fit."

Michael slammed him again. "Where's Gibril?"

"Behind you," Vaughan whispered.

Michael reacted on instinct – spinning, weapon raised.

A single Umbra operator stood ten metres away, rifle aimed.

But he didn't fire.

He dropped the rifle.

Then stepped back.

Then disappeared behind the smoke.

Michael turned back.

Vaughan was gone.

No footsteps.

No impact sound.

No shifting metal.

Gone.

As if the earth had swallowed him.

Seray reached him seconds later, breath sharp. "Where is he?"

Michael stared at the empty space where Vaughan had stood. "He ran."

"Through what, a wall?" Alhaji said, arriving behind her. "We had angles covered."

Michael wasn't listening. He knelt, picking up the fallen cane.

It wasn't Vaughan's usual one – heavier, reinforced, with a barely perceptible seam along one side.

He rotated it.

A panel clicked loose.

Inside was a microdrive.

Red.

Unmarked.

Seray let out a low whistle. "That's Consortium-grade."

Michael pocketed it. "Which means this wasn't an extraction."

"What was it then?" Alhaji asked.

Michael stood, staring at the wrecked Hilux, the shredded tyres, the phoenix-marked containers in the distance, the tunnel hatch still half open.

"A message," he said. "And an invitation."

The injured driver from the tunnel staggered toward them, supported by two ground crew Michael hadn't noticed emerging from the shadows. His face was pale, but his eyes were locked on Michael.

"They've gone inland," the man whispered. "More convoys. More people. Carted like… like cargo."

Michael gripped his shoulder. "Rest. We'll find them."

The man shook his head weakly. "They said… Redhawk is coming."

Michael inhaled slowly.

A storm gathering on the horizon.

A phoenix rising on shipping containers.

A mentor returned to play guide.

A cousin working in shadows.

A network preparing something vast and merciless.

And now–

Redhawk.

Seray wiped sweat from her brow. "What's the play?"

Michael looked south, toward the interior, toward the roads branching into the forests like veins feeding a heart none of them could yet see.

"We stop the next move," he said. "We find where those convoys are going."

"And after that?" Alhaji asked.

Michael closed his fists around the cane.

"We make the Consortium regret knowing my name."

He walked toward the rising sun, the others falling into step beside him, the airport behind them already swallowing the evidence of the morning's violence.

Ahead lay the forest.

The convoys.

Gibril.
Redhawk.
Truths no one survived learning.
Michael welcomed them all.
He wasn't running anymore.
He wasn't hiding.
He was hunting.

Chapter 10

THE BURDEN OF SILENCE

"The path you fear to walk is already watching your footsteps."
– African proverb

The forest pressed close around them, the air thick with the scent of damp earth and something older, something metallic beneath the soil. Dawn was still a rumour in the canopy, faint shafts of pale light filtering through leaves dense enough to smother the sky. Moisture clung to every surface, turning branches into slick ribs of shadow.

Michael moved first.

Seray was a step behind him, her breath steady despite the climb. Alhaji followed last, sweeping their rear with calm, deliberate discipline. The three of them advanced along the ridge trail – the quietest approach to the border zone, and the least forgiving.

They had been walking for thirty minutes before the first sign appeared.

A cigarette.

Freshly stamped out beside the path.

Michael crouched beside it, touching the ash.

"Still warm," he murmured.

Seray's hand went instinctively to her weapon. "We're being tracked."

"No," Michael said. "Someone's waiting."

Alhaji scanned the tree line. "Then they're confident."

Michael stood, eyes narrowing at the way the forest shifted ahead – not visibly, but in its silence, in the strange stillness that fell when predators occupied space meant for other things.

They reached a bend in the trail.

The man stepped into view.

Dillon.

Pressed uniform.

Imported boots.

Expression of bureaucratic superiority stretched thin over something more feral.

He held a notebook in one hand, his stance casual, as if he were inspecting a shipment rather than blocking a trail in the Guinean highlands.

"Morning," Dillon called. "I wondered how long it would take you to get this far."

Michael didn't answer.

Seray lifted her pistol slightly. "Bold of you to show your face without an escort."

Dillon smiled. "Who said I'm alone?"

Michael scanned the trees.

No movement.

No sound.

Too quiet.

Dillon flipped open the notebook. "You know, you really should stop visiting restricted areas. Samu isn't what it used to be. Neither are you, if we're being honest."

Michael took one step forward. "What do you want?"

"Want?" Dillon laughed softly. "Michael, I'm not here to want anything. I'm here to advise. If you walk another hundred metres, you'll cross an invisible line. And on the far side of that line…" He tilted his head. "Let's just say the people who operate there don't file incident reports."

Seray muttered, "Neither do we."

Michael ignored her.

"Why warn us?" he asked.

"Because you're useful alive," Dillon said lightly. "And because someone above my pay grade seems to think you still have a part to play. Personally, I disagree."

Michael's voice dropped. "You were at the airport."

Dillon's smile twitched. "It was a busy morning."

"You knew about the containers."

"Everyone knows about something," Dillon said. "The trick is knowing what not to know."

He closed the notebook with a soft snap.

"Turn around," he said. "Go back to Conakry. Have a beer. Pretend none of this is happening. Leave Samu alone."

Michael stepped closer, his voice low. "I did leave it alone once. Look what happened."

Dillon's expression shifted – just a flicker, just enough to confirm the man knew more than he was permitted to admit.

"You won't like what you find there," he said.

Michael took another step.

"So show me."

For the first time, Dillon hesitated. His eyes darted past Michael to the treeline behind.

A sound drifted through the forest.

Soft. Metallic.

The unmistakable click of a trigger being tested.

Seray snapped her gun upward. "Ambush!"

Michael pushed left, grabbing Seray by the shoulder and dragging her behind a fallen trunk as gunfire erupted from the ridge above. Alhaji dove the opposite direction, returning fire with disciplined bursts.

Dillon didn't flinch.

He simply stepped backward into the shadows, unhurried, untouched by the chaos around him.

"Last warning!" he called. "Do not go to Samu!"

Then he vanished into the trees.

Bullets ripped through leaves overhead, splintering branches. Michael returned fire, forcing two shooters to duck behind a rock shelf. Seray hit a third with a clean shot to the shoulder, sending him tumbling down the slope.

Alhaji shouted from the right flank, "Movement retreating! They're pulling back!"

Michael rose enough to catch sight of the ambushers slipping deeper into the forest – professional, coordinated, not bandits, not amateurs.

Umbra.

But the withdrawal was too tidy. Too fast.

A show of force, nothing more.

A warning, just like Dillon's.

Michael exhaled slowly, dust settling around him.

Seray knelt beside him. "He's scared. Dillon's not built for front-line."

"No," Michael said quietly. "He's built for instruction."

"Someone sent the message," Alhaji added. "He's just the courier."

Michael looked toward the direction Dillon had disappeared.

Samu lay beyond that ridge.

Waiting.

Wounded.

Holding its breath.

And someone – maybe Dillon, maybe someone above him – was desperately trying to stop Michael reaching it.

He rose to his feet.

"Let's go."

Seray frowned. "He told us not to."

"Exactly."

Michael stepped deeper into the forest.

The path behind them fell silent.

Ahead, the trees narrowed like a throat.

Samu was close.

And whatever had been built there – whatever had been burned, buried, or resurrected – was ready to speak again.

The forest thinned as they approached the ridge, the undergrowth giving way to an unnervingly open rise of scorched soil and blackened trunks. Samu had burned recently – too recently. The ash was still loose, drifting when the breeze shifted, coating Michael's boots as if the place recognised him and wanted to leave its mark.

The old OSD training compound sat shrouded in morning haze. The outline was still unmistakable: parade square, lecture block, armoury, assault house. Except now it looked skeletal – like a carcass left for scavengers.

Alhaji inhaled slowly. "I thought this place was abandoned years ago."

"It was," Michael murmured.

Seray swept her rifle across the horizon. "Then why the burn?"

"To hide what came before," Michael said. "And what's still here."

They advanced in silence.

The quiet was wrong – not the peaceful kind of quiet, but the hollow kind that followed violence. Even the birds kept their distance. Michael felt the familiar tension creeping beneath his skin – the one that had surfaced every time Samu had threaded its way into his life.

He approached the old drill square.

Footprints.

Not many. Not fresh. But deliberate.

Human.

Organised.

Moving in patterns.

"Someone's been surveying," he said.

He crouched beside the tracks. The indentations were uniform. Same weight class. Same stride. These were not looters. Not locals seeking scrap metal. These were operators.

Seray nudged a charred metal casing with her boot. "Two weeks old, maybe three."

Michael nodded. "They burned the surface to clean the slate."

"But why?" Alhaji asked.

Michael stood and pointed toward the far corner of the compound.

A single structure had not burned.

The old control hut.

Scorched around the exterior but untouched inside.

He walked toward it, stepping carefully over debris. The hut was a low concrete cube – once used for training live-fire oversight, now silent. The door creaked open under his hand.

Inside was darkness.

And light.

A red light – blinking faintly at the back wall.

Seray hissed, "Camera."

Michael's pulse tightened.

The camera was small, disguised inside a rusted vent grate. The LED blinked in a steady, patient rhythm. No dust on the lens. No heat damage. No spider webs.

Someone was watching.

Now.

Not weeks ago.

Now.

Michael gestured for the others to stay low. He stepped closer, examining the wiring. The device was modern, military-grade, powered by a concealed cell embedded in the wall cavity.

"Umbra?" Seray whispered.

"No," Michael said. "Umbra doesn't use this casing."

"Then who?"

Michael stared at the camera.

"Someone wealthier."

He pulled a combat knife and sliced the cable.

The red light died.

Alhaji exhaled. "Whoever was watching us just lost their feed."

"Good," Michael said. "Let them wonder."

But even as he said it, he felt the weight of the place pressing in – Samu remembering him, the walls holding ghosts he hadn't yet dealt with.

He moved deeper into the hut, brushing dust aside with the back of his hand.

Marks.

Scuffed lines on the concrete. Circular patterns.

He knelt again, tracing the grooves.

"Tripods," he murmured. "Three of them."

Seray frowned. "For what?"

"Surveying," Michael said. "Or cinematics."

"Recording?" Alhaji asked.

Michael nodded. "Mapping. Documenting. Blueprinting."

"Blueprinting what?" Seray asked.

"Something they're planning here," Michael said. "Or something they already built and tore down."

He stood again, eyes sweeping the ruined compound.

"This wasn't vandalism. It was staging."

Alhaji shivered. "Feels like walking through a crime scene long after the bodies are gone."

Michael didn't answer. His gaze had caught something near the far perimeter fence.

A scorch pattern.

Circular.

Perfect.

Too perfect.

He walked toward it.

As he came close, the truth settled in his stomach with a cold heaviness.

The burn marks weren't from a wildfire.

They were from a controlled ignition.

Accelerants.

Directional burn pattern.

Downwind shaping.

Seray caught up to him. "What are we looking at?"

"A cover-up," Michael said. "This whole compound didn't burn because of neglect."

He pointed at the ash.

"It burned because someone wanted Samu cleansed."

"Cleansed of what?" Alhaji asked.

Michael scanned the ruins.

Ghosts.

Mistakes.

Secrets.

"Evidence," he said.

He knelt and picked up a fragment of blackened metal. It had melted, warped, but not enough to erase the faint engraving on its edge.

Seray leaned in. "Is that…?"

Michael nodded grimly.

The phoenix.

"The Consortium was here," he said quietly.

Seray swallowed. "Then Dillon wasn't warning us for our sake."

"No," Michael said. "He was warning us because someone told him to keep us away – someone who didn't want us seeing this."

Alhaji looked at the camera husk. "Then what now?"

Michael turned toward the collapsed armoury at the edge of the square.

"We see what else they tried to burn."

He walked toward it, the others falling in behind him.

Samu had always been a fracture line in his life.

Today, it was something worse.

A message.

And the senders were watching.

The collapsed armoury looked like the ribcage of some long-dead creature, half-swallowed by earth and ash. Michael stepped over the twisted metal beams, careful not to disturb the unstable debris. Seray and Alhaji followed, each movement measured, controlled.

The roof had caved inward years ago – but the collapse wasn't random.

It had been guided.

Michael crouched, brushing aside soot with the edge of his boot.

Stone blocks beneath the debris had been positioned deliberately, shaped into a funnel. When the fire hit, the roof was engineered to fall inward, locking whatever had been inside beneath tons of melted steel.

"Intentional demolition," Michael murmured.

Seray studied the pattern. "They buried something."

Michael nodded. "Something they couldn't afford to leave behind."

He moved deeper into the wreckage, navigating the skeletal frame until he reached the one corner less damaged than the rest. A section of wall still stood – scorched, cracked, leaning under its own weight – but intact enough to display what had once been stencilled across its surface.

Words.

Charred almost beyond recognition.

Seray angled her torch. "Is that… French?"

Michael tilted his head, reading the faint outline beneath the scorch marks.

PROTOCOLE PHÉNIX – LOT 2

His stomach clenched.

While Seray and Alhaji processed the French, he felt a familiar, unwelcome echo ripple through him – a memory he had tried to bury, just as they had tried to bury this.

"Michael?" Seray asked softly. "What does it mean?"

He ran a thumb over the charred lettering.

"It means Samu wasn't just a training ground," he said quietly. "They were testing things here."

"What kind of things?" Alhaji asked.

Michael didn't answer immediately.

He stepped away from the wall and toward a half-buried steel case lying under a collapsed beam. The lid had warped in the heat but not enough to destroy the hinges. He cleared the debris and forced it open with a grunt.

Inside were fragments of circuitry. Not phones. Not radios.

Smaller. Cleaner.

Prototype components.

Stripped.

Scorched.

But recognisable.

Seray crouched beside him. "What the hell is this?"

Michael exhaled slowly. "I saw designs like this years ago. Before the coup. Before everything fell apart."

Alhaji frowned. "Military tech?"

"No," Michael said. "Worse."

He held up a fragment of metal – smooth, curved, the size of a coin. An engraving ran along the surface.

The phoenix again.

Smaller.

Different.

An early iteration.

Seray's brows furrowed. "So Samu was part of the Consortium blueprint?"

"Not part," Michael said. "A proving ground. They tested their earliest systems here – surveillance, tracking, behavioural augmentation, data profiling. And after they abandoned the prototypes, they burned the site to erase the evidence."

Alhaji straightened. "Then Dillon knew."

"He knew something," Michael said. "But Dillon's just a conduit. Someone above him – someone with reach – sanctioned this cleanup."

Seray scanned the compound again, jaw tightening. "They didn't want anyone connecting the phoenix shipments to Samu."

"They didn't want anyone connecting me," Michael murmured.

Seray turned sharply. "You?"

Michael reached into the case again.

Beneath the ruined circuitry lay a sliver of laminated material – fire-damaged, warped, barely holding together. But the photo printed on it hadn't been completely destroyed.

Mariama.

The image was old – taken during a community outreach exercise when she'd been working in offender reintegration. Michael felt the breath leave him, not violently, but with the quiet weight of a memory folding itself open.

Alhaji spoke gently. "Michael…"

He didn't move.

He traced the charred edge of the photograph with one thumb.

"She was involved," Michael whispered. "Not willingly. But they had her close enough to study. Close enough to use."

Seray's voice softened. "You don't know that."

He did.

He remembered conversations at the time – cryptic remarks Mariama had made about foreign consultants, strange equipment, unusual visitors to the outposts near Samu. He had dismissed it then as temporary turbulence – growing pains in a system that was always fragile.

He'd been wrong.

Dead wrong.

He slipped the fragment of her photograph into his pocket carefully, as though afraid it would crumble.

"We need to move," he said.

Alhaji nodded. "Back to the trail?"

"No," Michael said. "There's one place left."

Seray frowned. "Where?"

Michael pointed to the far end of the compound – past the old quartermaster hut, beyond the fire line, toward the building that had once served as Samu's administrative heart.

A structure too central to burn.

Too symbolic to erase.

Too important to leave untouched.

"The command office," he said. "If anything survived the purge, it'll be there."

Seray checked her weapon. "And if someone's watching us right now?"

Michael glanced back at the dead camera.

The blackened phoenix.

The ruined prototypes.

The photograph of Mariama burned but not destroyed.

"Then they already know we're coming."

He turned toward the command building.

The others followed.

Samu was no longer just a wound.

It was a warning.

And they were about to open it fully.

The command office sat at the far edge of the compound, half-swallowed by vines and ash, its concrete walls cracked but somehow still defiant – like an old soldier refusing to fall even after the battle had ended. The doorway was blackened, the metal frame warped by heat, but the structure remained intact.

Michael slowed as they approached.

"Something's wrong," Seray murmured.

Alhaji scanned the rooftops. "No movement. No heat signatures."

"That's what's wrong," Michael said quietly.

He stepped inside.

The air was cooler here, shaded from the sun, heavy with the scent of burned paper and mould. Dust motes drifted in slow spirals, catching thin beams of light breaking through the cracked ceiling. The floor was a mosaic of collapsed files, melted binder clips, and the charred remains of desk legs.

But the fire hadn't consumed everything.

In the far corner, a metal safe – scorched, dented, but unopened – lay half-buried under debris.

Michael crossed the room and brushed ash from its surface. "Help me clear it."

Seray and Alhaji shifted broken concrete aside until the safe lay fully exposed. The lock was heat-warped but functional. Michael pulled a multi-tool from his belt and began working the mechanism.

It clicked open with a reluctant metallic groan.

Inside were only three items:

A leather-bound ledger, edges blackened

A black USB drive wrapped in foil

A small evidence bag containing a thin metal disc – the size of a coin

Michael lifted the disc first.

The ouroboros symbol.

The serpent eating its own tail.

And beneath it:

0143

Seray exhaled. "Umbra tally."

Alhaji frowned. "One hundred and forty-three what?"

Michael answered before thinking. "Operators assigned to Redhawk."

A chill rippled through the room.

Seray stared at him. "That many?"

"It's a full unit," Michael said. "More than a unit. It means this isn't containment. It's expansion."

He placed the coin gently in his pocket beside the charred fragment of Mariama's photograph.

Then he picked up the ledger.

The pages were fragile, curling at the edges, but the ink inside had survived. Rows of dates. Locations. Inventory lists. And names – some struck through, some circled, some annotated with codes he recognised far too easily.

Seray leaned over his shoulder. "These are shipping numbers."

Alhaji pointed to a column. "And these–these look like personnel identifications."

Michael's pulse tightened.

He turned to the back of the ledger.

There, in heavy handwriting that cut through the page:

PHÉNIX – PHASE 2 CONFIRMED
TRANSFER TO COASTAL HUB APPROVED
CLEARANCE LEVEL: G.S.

Michael's blood ran cold.

"G.S...." Seray repeated softly. "Gibril Sillah."

Michael closed the ledger.

The room felt smaller – shrinking inward, pulling memory and fury into the space behind his ribs.

He forced himself to breathe.

Carefully, deliberately, he set the ledger aside... and reached for the foil-wrapped USB.

It was light. Too light.

Prototype casing.

Encrypted.

Purpose-built.

He held it between his fingers.

Before he could speak, the faintest buzz rose through the floor – subtle at first, then growing, vibrating through the walls.

Alhaji's eyes widened. "Drone."

Seray swore. "Multiple drones."

Michael moved to the shattered window.

Three drones approached from the east – black, angular, military-grade, each with a stabilised weapon mount glowing beneath the chassis.

Seray grabbed the ledger and USB. "We need to go. Now."

Michael nodded once. "West wall. The vines will cover us."

They sprinted from the command office as the first drone fired – a burst of micro-charges that tore through the doorway, sending concrete fragments exploding behind them. Michael ducked left, pulling Seray down just as a second burst strafed the ground where they'd been seconds before.

Alhaji shouted from the tree line. "On me!"

Michael grabbed Seray's arm. They ran.

The forest swallowed them as the drones tore above the treetops, branches shredding under the barrage. They didn't fire blindly – they were tracking, calculating, adapting.

Consortium drones.

Not Umbra.

Worse.

They reached a cluster of dense undergrowth, diving beneath heavy vines as one drone swept overhead, searching, scanning. Michael held his breath as the machine hovered only a metre above the canopy.

Seray whispered, "Why aren't they firing?"

"Because they're confirming," Michael murmured. "Not eliminating."

Alhaji frowned. "Confirming what?"

Michael answered without looking up.

"That we found the ledger."

The drone lingered. Listening.

Waiting.

Recording.

Then – abruptly – it banked away, retreating toward the burned perimeter.

The other two followed.

Seray exhaled shakily. "Why leave us alive?"

Michael wiped ash from his sleeve. "Because someone wants the next move to happen."

"And what's the next move?" Alhaji asked.

Michael gripped the foil-wrapped USB.

The metal disc.

The ledger.

G.S.

The phoenix burn.

Samu's cleansing.

"It's not here," Michael said. "Samu was the prelude."

He turned toward the forest path leading west.

"The real operation is along the coast."

Seray's jaw tightened. "Then that's where we go."

Michael stepped forward, eyes fixed on the fading drone hum – a sound that felt like a timer being wound.

"We leave now," he said. "Tonight we fly. Tomorrow we hunt."

Behind them, Samu burned silently in the morning light.

Ahead, the next fracture line waited.

The Consortium had taken the first move.

Michael intended to take the second.

And for the first time since Mariama's death, he felt something sharp and certain settle in his chest.

Resolve.

CHAPTER 11

THE SHADOW THAT WATCHES BACK

"Even the hunter becomes prey when the forest chooses to remember him."
– AFRICAN PROVERB

The hidden airstrip was barely more than a scar carved into the earth – a long, pale wound cut between the trees, its edges lined with rusted fuel drums that hadn't held fuel in years. A single hangar squatted at the far end, its corrugated walls blistered by the sun, the metal warped like old armour.

The place was quiet.

Too quiet.

Michael moved first, boots crunching lightly over the packed dirt, Seray and Alhaji flanking him in a wide, deliberate arc. The humidity wrapped around them like a second skin. No birds. No insects. No distant engines.

Just the static stillness of expectation.

Inside the hangar, a thin strip of light cut across the floor, highlighting dust motes twisting lazily like they were unsure whether they belonged to the air or the earth. Michael stepped inside–

And felt the shift.

Someone was here.

"Close the door," a voice said from the shadows.

Orion.

He emerged slowly, leaning on a simple grey walking stick – not ornate like Vaughan's, not a statement piece, but weathered, practical, and dangerous if he chose it to be. His face carried that familiar half-smile, the one Michael had once mistaken for warmth before he understood the truth: it was calculation wearing a mask.

"You took longer than expected," Orion said. "Age catching up to you?"

Seray lifted her pistol. "One more word and we'll see how fast you are."

Orion held up a hand, almost amused. "If you were going to shoot me, Seray, you'd have done it on the tarmac two days ago. You're loyal, but you're not reckless."

Michael ignored the provocation. "Why bring us here?"

"Because this is where the next decision begins." Orion waved his stick in a small arc. "Choice. Perspective. Alignment. The usual coming-of-age rites for a man who insists on rewriting his own fate."

Michael stepped closer. "Drop the performance."

Orion's eyes sharpened. "Still impatient. Still predictable."

"Still standing," Michael said.

"Not for long," Orion replied calmly. "Not if you keep digging in places designed to stay buried."

Seray stepped to Michael's side. "Talk. Now."

Orion studied her. "You're a good soldier. Loyal. Capable. But you're fighting a story that's already been written."

He turned back to Michael.

"You, however… you're a footnote that refuses to go quietly."

Michael didn't blink. "What's the Consortium doing in Matru?"

Orion clicked his tongue. "Straight to the plot twist. No build-up. You disappoint me."

"Answer the question."

"I'll answer a better one," Orion said. "Why you're still alive."

Michael's jaw tightened.

Orion leaned forward. "You think you've been avoiding them? You haven't. You've been protected."

Seray scoffed. "By who? You?"

"Don't flatter me," Orion said. "My loyalty is rented by the hour."

He tapped the stick once. "But there is someone who refuses to let you die."

Alhaji frowned. "Why?"

Orion shrugged. "Maybe he needs you. Maybe he respects you. Maybe he hates you so much he wants to kill you himself."

Michael felt the cold truth slide through him. "Gibril."

Orion smiled. "There he is. The ghost behind your shoulder."

Michael stepped forward, closing the distance. "Where is he?"

"Close," Orion said. "Very close. But you won't see him until he wants you to. That's his gift."

"Then why are you here?" Michael asked.

"To keep you from dying before he arrives."

Orion gestured broadly. "This airstrip is a crossroads. Your crossroads. Step the wrong way, and you won't live long enough for the next chapter."

Michael tightened his grip on his weapon. "What's in Matru?"

"A warning."

"What kind of warning?"

Orion's expression changed. Slightly. Enough to reveal something real beneath the mask.

"The Consortium is no longer experimenting," he said softly. "They are activating."

Seray felt her breath catch. "Activating what?"

Orion looked at Michael. "Everything Samu started. Everything Mariama stumbled into. Everything you've tried – and failed – to outrun."

Michael's stomach twisted at the sound of her name spoken in this place.

Orion saw the reaction and softened his tone, almost gently. "You think Mariama died alone? She didn't. She died inside the machinery you're chasing."

Michael's fingers curled slowly into a fist.

Before he could speak, a radio crackled somewhere outside the hangar – a faint burst of static carried on the wind.

Orion glanced over Michael's shoulder.

"You're out of time," he said. "If you stay here, they'll converge on you from three directions. If you leave now, you'll slip between them."

Michael growled, "You set this up."

"I nudged the dominos," Orion corrected. "But the direction they fall?"

He tapped his chest.

"That's all you."

A second burst of radio chatter filled the air.

Closer.

Organised.

Umbra.

Seray moved fast. "We need to go. Now."

Michael stared at Orion. "This isn't finished."

"It never is," Orion said with a smile.

Then he stepped back into the shadows and was gone.

Michael turned toward the open hangar doors as boots thundered in the distance.

He didn't hesitate.

"Move!" he shouted.

They ran into the forest as the first Umbra team stormed the airstrip behind them.

The shadow of the Consortium wasn't just watching anymore.

It was hunting.

They tore through the treeline, branches whipping across their jackets as the forest enclosed them in its dense, suffocating grip. The airstrip vanished behind them, swallowed by foliage and distance, but the echo of boots and radio static lingered like a phantom pressing at their heels.

Alhaji took point now, cutting a narrow line through the undergrowth, eyes sharp, breath steady. Seray stayed close behind Michael, scanning every angle, her tension a taut wire ready to snap.

They didn't speak for nearly a kilometre.

When Michael finally slowed, collapsing behind a fallen eucalyptus trunk slick with moss, Seray crouched beside him.

"You okay?" she asked.

"I'm thinking," he said.

"Same as asking if you're okay."

He huffed once – not quite a laugh, not quite a breath. "I'm fine."

Alhaji joined them. "We won't be for long if we stay on the ridge. Umbra will sweep it."

Michael nodded. "We go down."

Seray frowned. "Into the ravine? It's tight. Bad visibility."

"Exactly," Michael said. "Tight means they can't flank easily. And it leads toward the old smuggler paths."

"Where you and Gibril used to–"

Michael cut her off with a look.

She swallowed the rest.

They dropped into the ravine, sliding through the loose soil as the canopy above knotted tighter, blocking out most of the light. The air shifted – cooler, but heavy, as though the forest had exhaled something it had been holding back.

Roots twisted across the ground like veins. Standing pools reflected the trees in warped, restless fragments.

Seray whispered, "Feels wrong down here."

Michael didn't disagree.

He moved forward, careful of every foothold, until he reached an elevated slab of rock that formed a natural choke point. He paused long enough to listen.

Silence.

Too perfect to trust.

He knelt, brushing his fingers across the damp soil.

Tracks.

Three sets.

Fresh.

Moving fast.

Alhaji knelt beside him. "Ours?"

"No," Michael murmured. "We're not the only ones running."

Seray scanned the shadows. "Umbra?"

"Maybe," Michael said. "But these tracks are uneven. Not a squad. Not disciplined. Someone fleeing."

"Someone?" Seray repeated. "Or something?"

Michael didn't answer.

He pushed on.

The ravine curved sharply left, then tightened into a natural bottleneck where a large uprooted tree blocked half the passage. Michael ducked under it–

And froze.

Carved into the exposed root wall, hidden beneath a smear of mud, was a mark.

A circle.

Crossed once.

A sign he hadn't seen in years.

Seray saw it too. "What is that?"

Michael touched the symbol with the back of his hand, the way he had been taught long ago.

"It's a direction marker," he said quietly. "Old smuggler code. Means 'safe enough to pass, but don't linger.'"

Alhaji blinked. "And who uses it now?"

Michael stood. "Someone who wants to be seen by me."

"Gibril," Seray said.

Michael didn't confirm it aloud. He didn't need to.

They followed the ravine until it widened into a shallow basin. A thin stream ran through the centre, carrying the faint metallic scent of old iron deposits. On the far side, wedged half beneath a collapsed section of rock, was the entrance to a crawlspace.

One metre high.

Five metres across.

Pitch black.

Alhaji shook his head. "No way Umbra goes through that."

"Exactly," Michael said.

Seray knelt beside the gap. "You've used this before."

Michael didn't deny it. "It leads deeper into the plateau. It's cramped, but it opens out after fifty metres."

"And after that?"

Michael hesitated.

"Another fifty metres," he said. "Then a clearing."

Seray studied him. "You're sure?"

"I'm sure."

She didn't ask how he knew.

Michael ducked first, sliding into the crawlspace. The ceiling scraped the back of his shoulders, and the cold earth pressed tight around him, leaving barely enough room to breathe comfortably. The air smelled of damp soil, old stone, and something metallic lingering in the dirt.

He moved forward on his elbows, Seray close behind, Alhaji bringing up the rear.

Ten metres in, the darkness deepened, compressing around them like a fist. Dirt brushed Michael's cheeks. Stones scraped his forearms. His breath echoed between the narrow walls, amplifying the steady drum of his pulse.

Seray whispered behind him, "Michael? You good?"

"Yes."

But the crawlspace pressed memories against him he hadn't invited – Samu's shadow, Mariama's voice, the feeling of running through tunnels in a coup that had never truly ended.

At twenty metres, the ground dipped. A thin trickle of water seeped beneath them.

At thirty, Seray hissed, "Wait."

Michael paused.

A faint scraping noise ahead.

Not rock shifting.

Not animals.

Something else.

Movement.

Human movement.

Slow.

Deliberate.

Waiting.

Michael tensed. "We're not alone."

Seray's hand brushed his boot. "Do we back out?"

"No," Michael said. "We go forward."

The scraping stopped.

Michael switched off his torch and waited.

Seconds stretched.

Then a soft sound emerged from the darkness ahead – a voice, hoarse, barely audible.

"Michael..."

Seray's breath hitched. "Who–?"

Michael swallowed once.

He knew that voice.

Not Gibril.

Not Orion.

Someone else.

Someone from the old operations – someone he never expected to hear again.

The voice came again, frayed and raw.

"Michael... they said you'd come."

His skin prickled.

"Who are you?" he whispered.

A pause.

Then:

"The one they left behind."

The darkness seemed to pulse.

Seray whispered sharply, "Michael, this is a trap–"

But he knew it wasn't.

This was worse.

Not a trap.

A survivor.

Michael steadied himself, heartbeat steadying into an old, disciplined rhythm.

"Keep moving," he said. "Carefully."

They pushed deeper into the crawlspace, each metre drawing them toward the voice – and the truth buried beneath the forest.

Whatever waited ahead wasn't Consortium.

Wasn't Umbra.

It was something else.

A piece of the past that had crawled back to meet him.

The crawlspace widened abruptly into a shallow pocket of stone, like a hollow carved into the earth by time and pressure. Michael slipped into it first, crouched low, eyes adjusting to the muted glow bleeding in from a hairline crack in the rock above.

The man was there.

Curled against the back wall, half-covered in dirt, clothes in tatters, skin the colour of old parchment. His hair hung in matted ropes; his beard was streaked with soil. He looked starved, dehydrated, beaten – but the eyes were unmistakable.

Wide.

Alert.

Burning with a familiar, desperate intelligence.

"Michael…" he rasped again, voice raw from disuse.

Seray slid in behind Michael, gun up, breath halted in her throat. Alhaji followed slower, shock written across his features.

Michael crouched.

"Lamin."

The man closed his eyes, relief trembling across his ruined face.

"I knew… you'd come," Lamin whispered.

Seray shot Michael a sharp glance – not fear, but surprise. "You know him?"

Michael nodded, jaw tight. "He was part of the OSD liaison unit. During the coup. One of ours."

"He shouldn't be alive," Alhaji murmured. "We were told he died."

Lamin laughed – a fractured, broken sound that dissolved into coughing. "They told you… because they needed you to stop looking."

Michael leaned closer. "Who did this to you?"

Lamin looked up, and for the first time his eyes revealed not just pain, but trauma etched into every stare.

"The ones who came after Samu fell," he said. "They took me. Questioned me. Used me. Then left me here when I stopped being useful."

Seray frowned. "Umbra?"

Lamin shook his head slowly. "Umbra is just the muscle. These were different men. Men who never said their names. Men who watched everything… like it was a science experiment."

Michael felt the hair on the back of his neck rise. "Consortium."

Lamin's eyes flickered. "They never used that word. But they bore the phoenix."

He lifted a trembling finger to his left shoulder. Beneath a crusted layer of dried blood and dirt, a faint marking was burned into the skin – crude, improvised, but unmistakable.

A phoenix.

Not a symbol.

A brand.

Seray's breath caught. "Jesus."

Lamin shook in a small, involuntary shiver. "They marked everyone. Said it made us 'traceable'. Said no one leaves their chain."

Michael's stomach twisted.

"How long?" he asked.

"I don't know," Lamin whispered. "Time… time stopped mattering. Days. Weeks. Months. They kept moving me. First to the inland camps. Then to the forest. Then here."

Seray knelt beside him. "Why here? Why leave you alive?"

Lamin swallowed, voice trembling. "I became a test. They wanted to see if anyone would come."

Michael felt the implication like a punch.

"They were watching me," he said quietly.

Lamin nodded with a weak, fractured motion. "They said… 'He will return to the source. He always does.'"

Michael's breath slowed.

Alhaji looked horrified. "They used you as bait."

"No," Lamin whispered, his eyes finding Michael's with painful clarity.

"They used me as a mirror. To see what you'd do. To see who you'd become."

Michael closed his eyes briefly.

He had known Lamin. Trusted him.

They had patrolled Kambia together after the coup.

Shared food when supply lines broke.

Buried friends in the same shallow graveyard when the country fell apart.

Lamin had deserved better.

Michael opened his eyes. "We're getting you out of here."

"No." Lamin's voice sharpened with sudden fear. "You can't take me with you. They're watching. They always watch. If they see you helping me–"

Seray cut him off. "They've been watching since Samu. Since the airstrip. They already know."

Lamin shook his head violently. "You don't understand. This is what they wanted. This moment. This meeting. They want to see if you'll carry the weight."

Michael's voice softened. "Lamin…"

Lamin grabbed his forearm with surprising strength. "Listen to me. They aren't tracking you with drones. They're not tracking you with Umbra. They're tracking you with choices. Every decision you make is another page they read."

Seray frowned. "What does that mean?"

"It means," Lamin gasped, "they're predicting him."

Michael froze.

Alhaji whispered, "Predicting you how?"

Lamin's grip tightened. "Behaviour models. Psychological maps. Pattern loops. You think you've been chasing them? You've been walking inside a cage they built for you."

Michael felt something cold settle in his chest – not fear, but anger forged into something colder. Sharper.

"What do they want me to do now?" he asked.

Lamin let out a long, slow breath. "They want you to leave me."

Seray's eyes widened. "No."

Alhaji whispered, "That's monstrous."

"That's why they chose me," Lamin said softly. "Because they knew what I meant to you."

Michael looked at him – really looked – and saw the truth Lamin was carrying.

He wasn't scared of dying.

He was scared of what Michael would become if he broke the pattern.

Michael lifted him gently, hand behind his neck. "I am not leaving you."

Lamin's eyes filled with tears. "Then you're already inside their next move."

Before anyone could answer, the crawlspace behind them echoed with a faint sound.

A footstep.

Soft.

Deliberate.

Too controlled to be accidental.

Seray inhaled sharply. “Michael–”

He raised a fist. “Lights off.”

Darkness flooded the hollow.

Voices drifted from the tunnel.

Calm.

Measured.

Speaking in French-accented Krio.

Michael felt Lamin tremble.

“They’ve come back,” Lamin whispered. “They always come back.”

Michael steadied him.

“Then this time,” he said quietly, “they’ve come for the wrong man.”

He tightened his grip on his weapon.

In the darkness of the old crawlspace, three allies, one survivor, and a shadow from Michael’s past prepared for the next confrontation – silent, tight, and inevitable.

The voices in the tunnel grew clearer – soft, controlled, too calm for men moving into danger. Michael recognised the cadence immediately.

Not Umbra.

Not local militia.

Consortium field operatives.

Professionals who didn’t speak unless there was purpose in the sound.

Seray leaned close, whispering barely above breath: “Two. Maybe three.”

Alhaji angled his weapon. “Tunnel’s too narrow for a firefight.”

Michael agreed – a gun battle in a confined earthen throat would tear the place apart and leave Lamin buried. They needed space. They needed angles.

They needed to be smart.

He mouthed follow me, then slipped silently toward the left-hand alcove – a narrow fissure of rock he remembered from years ago, when this place had been used for cross-border smuggling and quiet escapes.

Seray guided Lamin gently into the nook, shielding him with her body. Alhaji took the opposite wall, rifle low but ready.

Michael flattened himself against the darkest shadow, listening.

The operatives weren't rushing.

They weren't hunting blindly.

They were advancing with the calm confidence of men who believed the situation was already won.

The first voice emerged through the dark:

"–movement ahead. Three, possibly four. Heat signatures faint."

A second replied:

"Proceed. Do not engage unless instructed."

Michael felt his pulse steady. Unless instructed meant these were observers, not executioners. They were here to watch outcome, not shape it.

Just like Lamin had said.

Predictive modelling.

Behaviour sequencing.

Watching Michael make a decision under pressure.

This wasn't a kill team.

This was an experiment.

Michael's jaw tightened. Enough.

He tapped the butt of his rifle once on the stone – a tiny click.

Seray heard it.

Alhaji heard it.

Lamin, trembling, heard it.

The operatives did not.

Michael waited until the footsteps were nearly at the chamber mouth.

Then he moved.

A burst of dirt and shadow as he launched forward, grabbing the first operative by the collar and dragging him violently into the stone wall. The man's head struck with a dull thud, his weapon clattering to the floor.

Seray lunged from the opposite angle, sweeping the second operative's legs out from under him. He hit the ground hard, breath bursting from his lungs.

Alhaji pinned him before he could recover.

Michael yanked the balaclava from the first man's face.

Young. Calm. Expressionless.

Consortium-trained.

"Why are you here?" Michael demanded.

The operative didn't answer – not with words. His gaze flicked once toward the crawlspace, then back to Michael.

A behavioural tell.

A reading.

A calibration.

They weren't here for Lamin.

They were here for him.

Michael's voice hardened. "Tell your masters this: I am not part of their model."

The operative exhaled once – not fear, not defiance.

Acceptance.

"Every choice," the man whispered, "is data."

Michael slammed him unconscious.

The second operative fought to breathe under Alhaji's weight. Seray leaned in, placing her knee on his chest.

"Speak," she said, voice cold. "Who sent you?"

He coughed once – a wet, humourless sound.

"You already know," he rasped. "The phoenix rises… where the old world falls."

Michael grabbed the man's flak vest. "Where's Gibril?"

The operative's expression shifted – marginally, but enough.

Michael felt something twist in his gut.

"He's close," the man croaked. "But not here. Not yet. He wants you to keep walking. Wants you to find what he left in the town by the coast."

Michael's breath slowed.

Bureh Town.

That was the next thread.

The next fracture line.

Seray looked at him. "Michael…?"

The operative suddenly reached for something inside his vest – not a weapon, but a charge trigger.

Michael reacted instantly, smashing his hand away and driving his elbow into the man's temple. Alhaji tore the trigger device free.

A dead man's switch.

Fail-deadly protocol.

"They were sent to erase themselves if caught," Alhaji muttered. "This is fanatic-level training."

"No," Michael said quietly. "This is conditioning."

He dragged both operatives into the side alcove and checked the tunnel.

Clear.

For now.

Seray steadied Lamin. "We need to get him out. He won't survive another hour down here."

Lamin's breath rattled. "You shouldn't… you shouldn't stay. They'll send more."

Michael knelt beside him. "We're taking you with us."

Lamin shook his head weakly. "Michael… don't let them use me against you."

"They already tried," Michael said. "And they failed."

Lamin's eyes softened – a flicker of who he once was. A man who had fought alongside Michael. A man who never deserved this fate.

"Then finish what we started," Lamin whispered. "End what Samu began."

Michael clasped the back of his neck, the gesture equal parts promise and farewell. "I will."

They manoeuvred him carefully back through the crawlspace, Michael taking point, Seray steadying Lamin's weight, Alhaji guarding their rear.

By the time they reached the ravine again, the forest was beginning to shift – wind funneling through the trees, carrying distant echoes of movement deeper up the plateau.

Umbra searches.

Consortium sweeps.

Drones repositioning.

The net was tightening.

As they reached higher ground, Lamin winced sharply. Michael halted.

"You alright?" he asked.

Lamin nodded weakly. "Just–just go. I can walk."

He couldn't. They all knew it. But the will in his voice mattered.

Michael lifted him gently.

Ahead, a break in the trees revealed the faint outline of a footpath leading west – toward the old smuggler routes, toward the coastal track, toward the next piece of Gibril's trail.

Seray secured her pack. "What's our next move?"

Michael looked down at Lamin – broken, branded, used.

Then toward the fading drone hum overhead – the sound of a machine waiting for him to choose.

"We take Lamin to the coast," Michael said. "Get him out. Get him safe."

"And after that?" Alhaji asked.

Michael stared into the forest.

"Bureh Town."

Seray nodded once, grim and certain. "Then let's move."

They slipped into the shadowed path, Lamin supported between them.

Behind them, the forest swallowed the crawlspace, the chamber, the operatives.

Ahead, the coastline waited – along with Gibril, the next phoenix, and the next escalation.

Michael didn't look back.

The Consortium wanted to read his choices.

Now he intended to write his own.

Chapter 12

THE FLARE IN THE DARK

"Those who bury truth in the sand
forget that the tide always comes."
– African proverb

Bureh Town lay beneath a low sheet of morning haze, the Atlantic pressing in with slow, deliberate breaths. Palms leaned inwards like eavesdroppers; rooftops of rusted tin glinted faintly through the shifting salt mist. The place looked abandoned to the casual eye – sleepy, harmless, content to let the world pass it by.

Michael knew better.

Places like this didn't grow quiet by accident.

He approached along the shoreline path, Seray at his shoulder, Alhaji sweeping the flanks. The surf rolled in behind them in heavy, rhythmic pulses – each one a low warning.

Ahead stood the mosque: whitewashed walls streaked with age, minaret leaning slightly as though bowing to the weight of years. Smoke rose from a makeshift fire pit outside, curling lazily into the air. But there were no voices, no children running across the courtyard, no call to prayer humming through the village.

Just stillness.

Michael paused.

Seray narrowed her eyes. "Feels wrong."

"Feels staged," Michael corrected.

They approached carefully. The mosque door creaked open at the slightest touch – not broken, not forced. Inviting.

Inside, the space was dim, shadows painted across the tiled floor. A lone figure sat near the rear wall, hunched forward, hands clasped tightly around a canvas pouch. His clothes were worn, his eyes hollowed by sleeplessness. Not old – but battered by whatever he'd been carrying.

When he looked up and saw Michael, something like recognition flashed in his expression.

"You came," the man whispered.

Michael didn't sit. "You signalled us."

The man nodded. "I had to. Before they came back."

Alhaji positioned himself by the door. Seray stayed near Michael, eyes scanning the prayer alcoves.

"What's your name?" Michael asked.

"Ismail."

"You're the contact?"

"I'm what's left of one," Ismail said bitterly. "The others… they're gone."

Michael crouched. "Tell me."

Ismail swallowed hard, hands tightening around the pouch. "A man came three nights ago. Gray hair. Tall. Moved like he owned the ground. Carried a cane he didn't need."

Orion.

Michael didn't let the reaction show on his face.

"What did he want?" Michael asked.

"To warn me," Ismail said. "Or to frighten me. Same thing with men like him."

Seray murmured, "Sounds familiar."

"He said," Ismail went on, "that a shipment was coming. Not the usual kind. Something… important. He said that when it moves, the world changes shape."

Michael exchanged a glance with Seray. This aligned exactly with what Orion had implied at the airstrip – activation, not experimentation.

"What else?" Michael asked.

Ismail hesitated before sliding the canvas pouch across the floor.

Michael opened it.

A hard drive. Scorched at the edges. Waterproof casing cracked as though it had been forced open. A sliver of metal still clung to its side – melted, curved, unmistakably shaped like a phoenix's wing.

Seray inhaled sharply. "Consortium-grade."

Ismail nodded. "He said you'd know what to do with it."

"What's on it?" Michael asked.

"I don't know," Ismail said. "I never plugged it in. I was told not to. He said it wasn't a message – it was a flare. Something to reveal who is watching."

Michael stared at the drive.

A flare.

Not information.

A reaction trigger.

"What happened after he left?" Seray asked.

Ismail's eyes shifted, haunted. "They came looking for it. The ones with the grey uniforms. Some Umbra. Some not."

"Consortium?" Michael pressed.

"I don't know the names," Ismail said. "But they weren't here to ask. They were here to check."

"Check what?"

"If the flare had been seen."

Michael stood slowly. "And did they see you?"

Ismail's silence was enough.

"He's burned," Seray murmured. "They marked him."

Michael nodded – the tension in the room thickening. Ismail's presence alone meant the Consortium had eyes on Bureh Town. If Orion had delivered the hard drive here on purpose, then everything inside this mosque was part of an instruction.

A behavioural test.

Another cage disguised as a choice.

Michael felt it.

Ismail's voice cracked. "I didn't mean for them to follow me. I thought… I thought you could stop it."

Michael exhaled once. "We'll try."

Seray stiffened. "Movement outside."

Alhaji slid back through the doorframe. "Two men at the end of the courtyard. Grey fatigues. Watching."

Michael picked up the hard drive, weighing it once in his palm.

The flare had already been lit.

He turned to Ismail. "We need to move. Now."

Ismail swallowed. "They'll kill me if they find me."

"They won't," Michael said, steady and certain. "Not while we're here."

Seray added under her breath, "But they will try."

Footsteps approached outside – not fast, not hurried.

Confident.

Expectant.

Michael slipped the hard drive into his jacket and stepped toward the courtyard door.

Seray covered him.

Alhaji raised his weapon.

Outside, the men in grey fatigues waited.

Watching.

Silent.

The Consortium hadn't come to stop him.

They had come to see what he would do next.

Michael stepped forward.

"I'm ready," he murmured – not to them, but to whatever shadow sat behind them, orchestrating.

He walked into the courtyard.

The chapter had begun.

The two men in grey fatigues didn't move as Michael stepped into the courtyard. They didn't reach for weapons. They didn't speak. They simply watched him with the same detached interest as scientists examining a specimen through glass.

That alone told Michael everything he needed to know.

These weren't hunters.

They were observers.

Sent to record his decisions.

Seray appeared at his flank. "We're leaving. Now."

The men didn't block their exit. They simply shifted weight – subtle, synchronised – like they were marking how Michael reacted to pressure.

Michael didn't give them the reaction they wanted. He walked past them as though they weren't there.

"Follow," he murmured to the others.

Seray guided Ismail out the side door, Alhaji circling to the rear to watch their back trail. They moved quickly, crossing behind the market stalls and slipping into the narrow path that led toward the mangrove edge.

The surf grew louder. The wind picked up, carrying a brine of salt and rotting vegetation. Burch Town's clustered houses gave way to a thin stretch of sand, then to the tangled, knotted mangroves that swallowed everything to the south.

Ismail stumbled on the uneven ground. Seray steadied him. "Stay with us."

Michael scanned the treeline behind them.

The grey-uniformed men hadn't followed.

Good.

Which meant something worse was waiting ahead.

They pressed deeper into the mangroves, the light fading almost instantly as the canopy closed overhead. The air thickened, humid and metallic. The ground sucked at their boots with every step, roots twisting like skeletal fingers beneath the mud.

Alhaji muttered, "Why does every trail you pick feel like a haunted one?"

Seray tapped him lightly. "Focus."

Michael slowed.

Just ahead, something hung from a low branch – a shape swaying gently, rhythmically, as if breathing with the tide.

Seray saw it too. "Wait."

Michael raised a hand.

They stepped closer.

It wasn't driftwood.

It wasn't debris.

It was a man.

Suspended by his ankles, body swaying over the stagnant creek. His chest was cut open, hollowed in a way that suggested interrogation rather than ritual. His face was slack, but his eyes – half-open – stared toward the village as though his final thought had been a warning.

Ismail recoiled, gagging. "He–he was one of the others. One of the contacts."

Alhaji whispered, "This was recent."

Michael studied the body.

No insects yet. No scavengers.

Hours old.

He scanned the perimeter.

"This was staged," he said. "Not torture. A message."

Seray swallowed. "For who?"

Michael looked at Ismail.

"For anyone protecting him," he said. "And for anyone he tried to contact."

Ismail's breathing quickened. "We shouldn't be here."

"No," Michael said. "We shouldn't stop."

They pushed on.

The mangrove density thinned until they reached a wider channel of water. A fishing canoe sat half-submerged near the bank – fresh cuts in the wood where someone had hacked at it to disable escape.

Someone had wanted to slow them.

Not stop them.

A behavioural funnel.

Michael clenched his jaw. “They're herding us.”

Seray's voice tightened. “Into what?”

Before Michael could answer, a soft rustling came from ahead – not human, not large enough for an armed squad, but close enough to make them all pivot.

A woman stepped from behind a screen of mangrove roots.

Barefoot.

Clothes stained with mud and charcoal.

Eyes bright with a survivalist alertness that belied her calm posture.

She wasn't armed.

She didn't look afraid.

“Which one of you is Michael Sillah?” she asked.

Seray stiffened. “Who wants to know?”

The woman pointed at Michael without hesitation. “You.”

Her accent carried a soft coastal lilt, shaped by Bureh dialect but sharpened by experience.

Michael lowered his weapon slightly. “Who are you?”

“Mariatu.”

Ismail nearly collapsed in relief. “She helped us–before the others were taken.”

Mariatu studied Michael with disarming directness. “You're late.”

Alhaji snorted. “This seems to be a theme.”

Michael stepped closer. “Why were they taken?”

“Because your friend” – she pointed at Ismail – “asked the wrong questions. And because men with money and uniforms don't like when villagers see too much.”

“What did you see?” Michael asked.

Mariatu gestured deeper into the mangroves. “Something was buried. Then something was dug up. Then something was moved in the night.”

Seray's eyes narrowed. “What?”

Mariatu met Michael's gaze.

“You're carrying the key to it.”

Her eyes dropped to his jacket – to the hard drive he'd taken from the mosque.

Michael exchanged a glance with Seray. "And what do you know about this?"

Mariatu didn't blink. "Enough to know they'll kill anyone near it. Enough to know that if you're still breathing, you need to leave now."

"Leave to where?" Alhaji asked.

Mariatu stared south, into the thickening wall of mangroves. "There's a shack. A safe one – for now. But after that…" She hesitated. "I don't think anywhere is safe."

Michael stepped closer. "How far?"

"Twenty minutes. If you don't stop."

"Then we move."

Mariatu nodded once, then turned and walked without waiting for permission.

Ismail followed her with fear etched into every movement. Seray stayed at Michael's shoulder. Alhaji covered the rear.

Michael glanced once at the hanging body behind them – swaying, watching, warning.

Then he followed Mariatu into the tightening throat of the forest.

The trap hadn't sprung yet.

But the pressure was building.

Mariatu moved fast for someone who had clearly endured too much. Her bare feet found every firm patch of mud, every knot of stable root, every silent stepping point worn into the mangroves by generations of coastal fishermen. Michael followed closely, reading her instincts, trusting them more with each passing minute.

The canopy thickened until daylight became a dull green haze. The path narrowed into a twisting corridor through walls of tangled roots and hanging vines. The smell of brine, rot, and sap merged into a dense, earthy heaviness.

"Almost there," Mariatu whispered.

Michael kept scanning left and right. "How do you know this place?"

"I was born here," she said. "I left once. The place didn't leave me."

Alhaji muttered, "Seems like a theme with this country."

Seray shot him a sharp look. "Eyes up."

The mangrove corridor widened suddenly, revealing a small clearing where a single shack leaned against the trees – zinc roof half-rusted through, walls patched with driftwood, netting, and what looked suspiciously like parts of an old canoe. Smoke stains marked the top vents, but no fire burned now.

"Inside," Mariatu said.

Michael motioned the team forward. He swept the shack's interior first: crude wooden table, overturned bucket, stacks of fishing line, and a narrow sleeping mat. It was empty. Recently vacated.

Too recently.

"Someone's used this as a relay point," Seray whispered.

Mariatu nodded. "The man before you. The one with the cane."

Michael stiffened.

"Orion?" he asked.

Mariatu's eyes flickered – recognition, but also something quieter. Unease. "He came through here at dawn. Told me to wait for you. Told me not to be afraid when the forest grew quiet."

Seray cursed under her breath. "He staged this."

Michael clenched his jaw. "He engineered every direction we've taken so far."

Mariatu frowned. "I don't know about engineering. But he said the same thing he said last time he came."

"What?" Michael asked.

Her voice dropped.

"That this place wasn't a trap… it was a test."

Michael's breath stilled.

Seray whispered, "He's playing you."

"No," Michael said. "He's predicting me."

Ismail collapsed onto a stool, exhausted. "Can we rest? Just a moment?"

"No," Michael replied sharply. "We can't stop."

But it was already too late.

The forest had gone silent.

No wind.

No insects.

No water movement.

Just stillness.

A stillness engineered.

Michael spun toward the treeline. "Positions. Now."

Seray dragged Ismail behind the shack. Alhaji dropped to a knee behind a fallen branch pile. Mariatu took cover inside the doorway, eyes sharp, jaw set with the fierce composure of someone who'd faced danger before and survived it.

Michael knelt behind a thick root, weapon steady, breath even.

The trap had sprung.

Something moved in the mangroves – soft, deliberate, perfectly coordinated. Shadows slipped between the roots and branches with eerie precision.

"Umbra?" Alhaji whispered.

Michael shook his head.

"No. This is cleaner."

The first flash came from the right – muzzle flare behind tree cover, followed by a suppressed crack. Bark exploded next to Michael's face.

He rolled left. Seray returned fire, forcing two shadows back.

Mariatu's voice cut through the chaos: "Three to the west! One circling!"

Michael flipped the selector switch on his weapon and fired two controlled bursts. A figure dropped instantly – tactical vest, grey fatigues, Consortium insignia sewn low on the hip.

Not Umbra.

Hybrid team.

A new detachment.

The air thickened with movement, branches snapping under the weight of advancing operators. Michael aimed again, heart beating in a controlled rhythm – not panic, not adrenaline.

Cold clarity.

Another suppressed shot hit the shack's doorframe, splintering wood. Mariatu ducked, rolled, and grabbed a fallen machete from the floor, moving with the quiet precision of someone who had lived her life on her own terms.

Alhaji fired a short burst. "They're trying to flank!"

Seray called out, "Pull back to the deeper roots!"

"No," Michael ordered. "We hold. We break their line here."

He pivoted, sighted, fired – centre mass. A second operative collapsed.

Another shadow slid along the treeline, low, fast, almost animalistic. Michael adjusted angle, squeezed the trigger, dropped him mid-step.

Something inside him shifted.

This wasn't reactive anymore.

He wasn't scrambling to survive.

He wasn't improvising.

He was calculating.

He was predicting them.

A grenade rolled toward the shack.

"Down!" Seray shouted.

Alhaji kicked it back into the mangroves. It detonated mid-air, sending a burst of mud and leaves over their heads.

The shockwave rattled Michael's bones. He steadied himself instantly.

"Two left," he murmured.

Alhaji blinked. "How do you–"

Michael had already moved.

He sprinted low across the mud, sliding behind a thick root, firing twice. One operative fell instantly, rifle clattering into the creek.

The final one hesitated – a fraction of a second too long – trying to read Michael's trajectory.

Michael fired first.

The clearing fell silent again – not the manufactured silence from before, but the hollow aftermath of violence.

Mariatu rose slowly, breathing hard but steady. "Is it over?"

"For now," Seray said, lowering her pistol.

Michael scanned the bodies. These weren't standard hunters. Their gear was cleaner, lighter, more specialised. These were field behaviour technicians – the ones who monitored elite predictive sequences.

Sent here to observe him up close.

Alhaji wiped sweat from his brow. "I count nine. How many did you expect?"

Michael didn't answer.

He stood at the edge of the clearing, listening to the forest.

Waiting.

Thinking.

This wasn't just survival.

It wasn't even a chase anymore.

This was a threshold.

And Michael had just stepped over it.

Mariatu approached him cautiously. "Why did they come for you?"

Michael didn't look at her. He stared into the mangroves, jaw hardening.

"They didn't come to kill me," he said quietly.

"Then why?"

"To see if I'd become what they think I am."

Mariatu shivered. "And did you?"

Michael exhaled slowly.

"No."

He holstered his weapon.

"But I think I'm becoming something they didn't plan for."

The clearing still trembled from the shock of gunfire – leaves settling, smoke drifting in thin grey ribbons, mud rippling with the last vibrations of violence. The bodies of the Consortium field team lay scattered among the mangroves, half-submerged in creek water, their grey fatigues already soaking into the swamp like they'd always belonged there.

Mariatu watched Michael as he scanned each corpse with cold, surgical attention.

"You've seen soldiers before," she said quietly. "This is different for you."

Michael didn't look up. "These aren't soldiers."

"What are they then?"

Michael rested on one knee beside the last operative. "Sensors."

Seray frowned. "Meaning?"

"They weren't here to win," Michael said. "They were here to measure."

Mariatu shivered. "Measure what?"

Michael stood, wiping mud from his hands. "How far I'd go."

Alhaji's eyes widened. "And?"

Michael didn't answer immediately. But the look in his eyes – steady, sharpened, deeply controlled – said everything.

He wasn't running anymore.

He wasn't hiding.

He wasn't reacting.

He'd stepped outside their prediction loop.

He had become unpredictable.

Mariatu moved closer, voice low. "We can't stay here. Others will come."

"Yes," Michael said. "But not yet."

He looked around the clearing. "This was the test group. The ones after us will be the clean-up team."

Seray nodded grimly. "Real military."

"We won't be here when they arrive," Michael said.

He turned to Ismail, who sat trembling against the shack wall. "Can you stand?"

Ismail nodded weakly. "I… I think so."

Mariatu helped him to his feet.

Seray leaned close. "Where now?"

Michael stepped into the centre of the clearing, listening to the forest, feeling the shift in the air – the subtle change in pressure that always followed violence in places like this.

"East," he said. "To the ridge."

Alhaji squinted. "What's on the ridge?"

"A vantage point," Michael said. "And if we're lucky… blistering sunlight."

Seray raised an eyebrow. "Why would sunlight help?"

Michael glanced at her.

"Because I need to see what's following us."

They left the clearing and ascended through the mangroves until the trees thinned and the ground rose sharply. The salty air thickened with heat. The canopy broke open to reveal a jagged ridgeline overlooking Bureh Town and the expanse of rolling Atlantic beyond.

Here, sunlight poured onto them like molten steel. The wind pulled smoke and humidity off their clothes.

It was a place meant for clarity.

Mariatu wiped sweat from her neck. "Now what?"

Michael scanned the horizon. "Where's your nearest evacuation point?"

"Further south," she said. "Past the old fisheries. There's a footpath that leads to the transport boats."

"Good." Michael pointed to Alhaji. "Take Ismail with her. Move now."

Alhaji hesitated. "And you?"

"Seray and I will follow."

Mariatu studied him. "Are you sure?"

Michael didn't respond with words – only a steady nod.

Alhaji gripped his shoulder. "Don't die here."

"Not today," Michael said.

They disappeared down the southern trail, Mariatu guiding Ismail with quiet urgency.

Seray stepped beside Michael. "You're waiting for something."

"Confirmation."

She looked at him. "Of what?"

Michael nodded toward the mangroves below.

On the far edge of the clearing they had just left, three black-armoured figures emerged from the shadows. Taller, bulkier. Faces masked. Movements disciplined.

Umbra.

True Umbra.

Tier-One.

Not observers.

Not testers.

Executioners.

Seray whispered, "Jesus."

Michael exhaled – not fear, not tension. Something colder. Calmer.

"They're late," he said.

"Late?" Seray hissed. "Michael, those are the ones sent to kill you."

"Yes," he murmured. "And Orion knows I saw them before they saw me."

Seray stared. "You think he planned that too?"

Michael shook his head. "No. That wasn't his plan."

He watched the Umbra operators kneel in the clearing, scanning the bodies, analysing the bullet patterns, reconstructing the fight. One pointed toward the trail Michael had taken. Another touched a device strapped to his forearm.

A signal.

Or a question.

Then, one by one, the operators turned – not toward the ridge, not toward the escape trail.

But toward the coast.

Seray frowned. "Where are they going?"

Michael closed his eyes briefly.

"That's the confirmation."

"Of what?"

"That they're not following me," Michael said quietly. "They're following the flare."

Seray's breath caught. "The hard drive."

"Yes."

Michael opened his eyes. "The Consortium didn't send Umbra to kill us. They sent Umbra to retrieve what they thought I'd run with."

Seray realised it at the same moment he spoke the next words.

"They expect me to panic," Michael said. "They expect me to flee south with Ismail and Mariatu. They expect me to run directly into their next net."

Seray turned to him slowly. "So what are we going to do?"

Michael watched the Umbra team vanish into the treeline, moving with the precision of men absolutely certain of their quarry.

"We break their model."

He reached into his jacket, pulled out the hard drive, held it once in the sunlight…

…and placed it gently on the ridge rock.

Seray blinked. "You're leaving it?"

"No," Michael said.

"We're using it."

He stepped back.

Sunlight glinted off the metal casing – a bright flash, sharp and visible for miles.

A flare.

A real one this time.

Below, the last Umbra operator paused, turning his head slightly – as though sensing the glint.

Seray exhaled. "You're drawing them here."

Michael's jaw hardened. "I'm showing them I know they're watching."

He turned south.

"We move."

They left the ridge just as the first Umbra operator began to climb.

Behind them, sunlight danced across the hard drive.

Ahead of them, the coastline curved toward whatever waited next.

The Consortium thought they had mapped his behaviour.

Now he intended to redraw the map.

EPILOGUE

London rain came at an angle–sideways, needling, the kind that made the whole city hunch its shoulders as though bracing for a truth it didn't want to hear. Michael stood beneath the narrow shelter of the archway outside the Foreign Office, watching the pavement gleam like a sheet of black glass.

He had expected distance to dull the echoes of West Africa. It hadn't. The city felt smaller now, its noise thin, its people rushing past without seeing the shadows they walked in. Sierra Leone had changed him. The Consortium had sharpened him. And the truth he carried felt heavier here, where everything pretended to be orderly.

A man approached through the curtain of rain–charcoal suit, polished shoes already ruined by the weather, expression as unreadable as granite. He moved with bureaucratic purpose, the kind that suggested rank without revealing it.

"Mr Sillah," the man said, offering a handshake that was purely procedural. "Thank you for coming in. Unofficially, of course."

"Of course," Michael replied.

They walked together beneath the overhang. The man did not offer a name.

"There's concern," he began, "that certain… activities in Sierra Leone may have exceeded the expected parameters."

Michael almost laughed. "Is that the new phrase? Parameters?"

The man ignored the remark. "Intelligence suggests multiple foreign actors were operational in the region. Some we predicted. Some we did not. We're trying to assess which category you fall into."

"I don't work for foreign actors."

"That's what worries us."

A black car pulled up to the curb, its engine too quiet to be government-issue. The man continued:

"You were instructed to return. You did. You were told to debrief. You did not. You were asked to account for your movements. You declined."

Michael met his gaze. "If you'd seen what I saw, you might decline too."

The man studied him with a clinical detachment that reminded Michael–uncomfortably–of Consortium field observers.

"We don't have the luxury of vague answers," he said. "Not with what's coming."

"And what is coming?" Michael asked.

A pause.

Then:

"Something old. And something new. And – forgive the language – something we have no name for yet."

Michael looked out at the rain, watching it hammer the pavement in relentless sheets.

The man adjusted his coat. "We'll be in touch. I suggest you make yourself reachable."

He stepped into the waiting car. The door shut with a sound that felt too final for a simple conversation. The vehicle slid away into the grey, vanishing into traffic like it had never been there.

Michael remained under the archway, hands in his pockets, rain misting the edge of his jacket.

He thought of Lamin.

He thought of Mariatu.

He thought of Gibril in the shadows, waiting for his next move.

And he thought of the phoenix–burned into metal, rising from ash, watching.

London felt colder suddenly.

Not because of the rain.

Because of the truth waiting beneath it.

Whatever was coming, the Consortium was already ahead. And Michael was done being a piece they tried to predict.

He stepped out into the rain.

Time to decide which bridges would burn next.

COMING SOON IN THE STRATEGIC SHADOWS SERIES

BOOK TWO – *The Shadow Cartography*
(Forthcoming)
As unseen networks of influence shift beneath the surface, Michael Sillah is drawn into a dangerous web of covert loyalties, hidden maps of power, and betrayals reaching far beyond Freetown.

BOOK THREE – *The Matru Protocol*
(Forthcoming)
A long-buried agreement resurfaces in one of Sierra Leone's most remote regions, pulling Sillah into a lethal struggle over tradition, authority, and the shifting balance of power.

BOOK FOUR – *The Fire Before Dawn*
(Forthcoming)
Instability threatens to engulf West Africa, forcing Sillah into a desperate race against ruthless forces determined to ignite chaos before the world wakes.

BOOK FIVE – *Title to be Announced*
(Forthcoming)
The Strategic Shadows deepen… and the truth grows more dangerous.

Printed in Dunstable, United Kingdom

75761331R00104